Fishcakes at the Ritz

Best Wishes Sylvia

Fishcakes at the Ritz

JUDY CORNWELL

Judy Cornwell

LONDON
VICTOR GOLLANCZ LTD
1989

First published in Great Britain 1989
by Victor Gollancz Ltd,
14 Henrietta Street, London WC2E 8QJ

© Judy Cornwell 1989

British Library Cataloguing in Publication Data
Cornwell, Judy
 Fishcakes at the Ritz.
 I. Title
 823'.914 [F]

 ISBN 0-575-04439-X

Photoset in Great Britain by
Rowland Phototypesetting Ltd, Bury St Edmunds, Suffolk
and printed by St Edmundsbury Press Ltd
Bury St Edmunds, Suffolk

*For Carol, Roz, Joan and André
with love*

PART ONE

Chapter One

Gloria watched the blonde waiting by the toilet. Couldn't she see it was vacant? She was probably too stoned. When Gloria joined the flight at Kennedy she had noticed the sprawled figure occupying two seats. She was high on free champagne then. That was more than five hours ago. Aware of the danger to herself, Gloria had watched with morbid fascination while continual requests were made for refills. But she had not succumbed to any temptation herself. Steve would be proud of her. An air hostess stopped by the toilet and opened the door. The young woman threw back her long hair and laughed. She looked like a kid but was probably in her mid-twenties, Gloria thought. She was wearing faded jeans with a sweatshirt and was not much taller than she was. Steve always joked about his little five-footer. His brown-eyed mouse.

She looked out of the window to the ground below. It really was as green as Steve had described it in his last letter. Small fields seemed stitched together like a shaded patchwork quilt. She closed her eyes and tried to picture Steve's face but could only see him as he was twelve years ago, when they were first married. She had been thirty then. Now it was nineteen seventy and she could not remember being forty or forty-one. Those years had been erased from her memory. She tried to search her mind for some event that would give an outline of her lost time but like a last sliver of moon dissolving in the sky, any glimpse into the past quickly faded. The depression began to creep back. What had the doctor said? "Gloria, don't try to remember. Just live for today."

She lit a Gauloise and stretched her right leg hard to prevent a muscle spasm. Dublin was only ten minutes away. Would it be different in Ireland? she wondered. Steve had promised it would be. She touched her hair nervously. It had been given a silver rinse and lacquered into a pageboy, just how he always liked it. She had got thinner since he last saw her. When she was weighed two weeks ago, the scales showed ninety-two pounds. She felt her ears go as the plane lost more altitude. Nervously she smoothed the wrinkles from her fine leather gloves as the wheels touched down on the runway.

It was draughty in passport control. Gloria pulled up her mink collar and tried to hide her shaking face in the dark fur. A porter rescued her from the confusion round the conveyor and his friendly conversation calmed her as they crossed to the customs counter. The blonde who had been on the plane was already there behaving outrageously with the young customs officer whose ears were pink with a mixture of embarrassment and pleasure. Gloria found herself chuckling. The broad looked a sight. She had put on dark glasses and was wearing a silver fox fur over her jeans. On her feet were floppy moccasins which could be picked up for a song in Elvira Street in L.A. All her bags were the cheap Schwaabs zip bags which were now opened to reveal utter chaos.

As Gloria came out of the customs hall she could see Steve's slight, drooping frame. His brown eyes searched anxiously for a glimpse of her among the arrivals. He held a wilting bunch of violets which he tapped absentmindedly against his coat.

"Steve."

Smiling with relief, he straightened his shoulders and made his way over to her.

"Welcome to Ireland, Mouse." His soft Brooklyn drawl was a promise of security against the painful world. He cautiously scrutinised her face for any signs of a lapse.

"I've been a good Mousey." She clung to him, breathing in the rough scent of tweed and recently applied aftershave. Nightmares were banished as she absorbed strength from the warmth of his skin. This time it had to be better. This time she had to make it.

Not even her strong tinted glasses could give colour to the grey January sky. The cold penetrated the muscles in her right leg so that the painful twitch returned. As she limped towards the Mercedes, the chauffeur hovering expectantly by the car stubbed out his cigarette and appraised her mink-clad appearance with hungry reverence.

"Good morning Mrs O'Connell." She noticed he carefully avoided registering any signs of disappointment as she drew nearer. There was his type all over the world, she thought. Always waiting for her at stations or airports. They sold their loyalty to the highest bidder.

"Hi! What do they call you?"

"Michael, Mrs O'Connell." His shrewd eyes weighed up the future possibilities of their relationship. Her blank stare unnerved him. He hurried round to the boot of the car, politely assuring her that Steve would be a lot happier now that she had arrived.

While Gloria's luggage was being loaded into the Mercedes, an explosion of flashlights greeted the young blonde who was emerging from the airport entrance. She began posing and smiling for the waiting group of photographers. The whoops of approval from the photographers caused Gloria to wheeze into laughter. She watched with admiration the way the young blonde handled the shouting men. As if sensing her gaze, the younger woman turned in her direction and grinned.

Gloria experienced a moment's bitter, sweet yearning. She too had been surrounded by photographers when she had first met Steve. New York's blonde Deb of the year had been exactly like this kid, giggling and flirting with all the fellows. She had been covered in white tulle, her mother's pearls resting on her bursting bosom. The hired publicity guy had stood bawling at the press as if they had not been welcome, despite mother's investment in promotion. Steve had appeared from nowhere and much to the family's rage led her on to the dance floor. In his shabby suit among the well-attired young bucks, he had been the dangerously exciting entity from the other side of the tracks. It was love at first sight. He had been married then. She frowned as memories of rows after the dance and vomit over the tulle spoilt the sweet reverie.

"You're Gloria." The large PR woman in charge of the operation bore down on them and seized Gloria by the fingers.

"This is Rachel Myers, dear. She's with American World Pictures."

"We know each other from Hollywood days," the woman shouted, "when I was with the Lazlo studios and Steve was with Reuters."

Gloria watched the small moustache over Rachel Myers' mouth and wondered whether the hearty upper class accent was cultivated to impress Americans. She glanced at the clothes adorning the stout figure and decided it *was* cultivated. She had never met an English dame from any of the old families who knew how to dress and this noisy cow had taken a great deal of care over her accessories.

"Isn't it a small world?" Rachel went on. "I never expected to see Steve here in Ireland. We bumped into each other the other day at Ardmore Studios and he told me you were going to live here."

"Yeah," said Gloria. "It's better for tax." She lit a Gauloise and watched Rachel gush film set gossip at Steve. "Who's the gal?" she interrupted. The woman sighed.

"Sophie Smith. She's hot at the moment. Just finished shooting *Cinderella Girl* in L.A." She paused and glanced back at her charge. "Right now, she's bombed out of her skull." Her anxiety caused the accent to slip. Gloria smiled. "I suppose I had better get back to her before she says something outrageous. This is a very Catholic country, you know." She started to stride towards the photographers but paused and adopted an almost childish stance while she asked them whether she could be invited to their house. Steve assured her she would, much to Gloria's disgust.

The Mercedes took off. Glancing through the rear window, Gloria caught sight of Sophie being bundled into a Rolls Royce. Her sunglasses were slightly askew. Some of the young girl's rebellion prodded Gloria's darker nature, reawakening the hatred for order and authority.

Through great iron gates and at the end of a long conifer-lined, gravel driveway, stood De Courcy House. The Mercedes halted before an ivy-covered entrance arch, over-shadowed by a large horse chestnut tree.

"Jesus, Steve," Gloria exclaimed in horror, "couldn't you find anything bigger?" She allowed herself to be assisted out of the car.

"Isn't this something?" Steve stood proudly waiting to show her the sombre estate. Behind him, neat lawns sloped to encompass an expanse of Black Rock Bay.

"I hope this is rented and not bought."

"Rented, dear."

Gloria felt spiky. Surely Steve hadn't begun to take his Irish ancestry seriously. That was a privilege for politicians.

Mary, toothless and cheerful, appeared at the door. The

housekeeper's red hands kneaded her flowered pinafore in anticipation of a greeting.

"Next to her, I look like Miss World."

Steve smiled patiently.

"She's no beauty, that's for sure, but she's O.K."

"Did you hire her to make me feel good or something?" Gloria hissed.

"Now dear . . ." He was interrupted as three excited dachshunds greeted Gloria. Ignoring the housekeeper's outstretched hand, she collapsed on to the hall floor and allowed them to crawl all over her.

Lottie was her favourite. Twelve years ago, Steve had given the puppy to her as a welcome back present when she had been discharged from Belle Vue. Ninka and Baby were her pups. Tears of guilt trickled from behind the dark glasses. She had hardly thought about the dogs during the nightmare days. All she had been concerned about was her own survival. Lottie nuzzled lovingly against her face.

"Mind the dogs don't ruin yer lovely coat, Mrs O'Connell."

It was that same tone of voice, the same condescending sound that echoed in every hatch. Jesus Christ! She was forty-two going on eighty. How dare this toothless Irish woman tell her what to do. The thrill that she had felt on seeing the dogs was replaced by an uncontrollable anger. The shaking began in the spine and vibrated through to her limbs. Still clutching the wriggling Lottie, she staggered to her feet, rejecting all Steve's attempts to help her. She tried to form the words but they came out slurred and incoherent. The rasping noise informed them that she was tired and wanted the bedroom.

As Steve led her up the broad staircase, black depression seeped into her mind. She saw the palatial bedroom. He had really surpassed himself with this joint. She glared at the four

14

poster and crackling log fire. It was like a set on an old British movie.

"Isn't it romantic, Mouse?"

"Yeah, but it's going to be a bit cold for my baby dolls."

Long nights in the units had taught her to discreetly observe the nocturnal habits of others. Carefully regulating her breathing, she lay as still as an alligator while her slit eyes watched Steve searching through her bags. Her inner self cried as her befuddled brain grasped the reality of her own vulnerability. She wanted to shout out, "I've been a good girl, Steve, I promise. I haven't taken one goddam pill. Yeah, sure I've kept a few. They're in the Tampax. But I've only kept them in case the going gets really rough. Please believe me. I haven't had any."

He crept quietly out of the room. Soft rain pattered against the window. Answering rivulets of self pity wet the pillow. Why did the reality never live up to her fantasies? Waiting for the days to pass before her release, she had planned their reunion. It should have been so different. Ireland was to have been a beautiful, green place with laughing, singing people. Steve would have met her at the airport and she would have been thirty again. They would have gone to a corn field and made love on silk sheets.

She had felt so randy on the plane. Apart from a quick bang with one of the male aides for a bottle of whisky, three months ago, she had been celibate and faithful to Steve. Her thin fingers searched her body for any sign of life. The dry skin flinched against her long nails. She was numb. From the tip of her bleached head to her nerve-damaged toes. She was a worn out, dried up husk. More tears ran down her chin.

What had the shrink told her?

"Don't project," he had said. Oh Jesus, how she projected. Her memory clung to the message given at the group therapy session. A day at a time. No self pity. She tried to remember more of the slogans but the effort of concentration exhausted her. She entered familiar oblivion.

*

Sophie opened her eyes to pitch black space. She reached for the familiar light switch. It wasn't there. Her heart thumped loudly and her skin broke into a cold sweat. She wondered whether she was having the recurring dream that always paralysed her vocal chords or whether she really wasn't in the Beverly Rodeo Hotel. Between dancing globules of shadow, there appeared a chink of light. Whimpering with fear she crawled across unfamiliar carpet and clutched at coarse, tweedy curtains. Outside she saw, not Rodeo Drive with the sleek Cadillacs passing the luxury beauty salon opposite, but a dark rain-washed street. Dingy cars weaved past muffled pedestrians. Of course, she was in Ireland and this was the Hibernian. The panic subsided. The dreams had not caught up with her. It was just the effect of the time change. She found the switch and filled the bedroom with welcome light.

Her cigarettes and watch were in the wastepaper basket. Ten o'clock and she was wide awake. She found the schedule on the floor and stared at it balefully. The car was to collect her at seven a.m. for hair and make-up tests. There was a coaching session with someone called Seamus Lynch at twelve noon and lunch with Fran Golder from Movie World. She knew Fran from past interviews. It would be an easy lunch. Sophie made a mental note to ask Rachel whatsit to find out the name of Fran's husband. He was a stamp collector or something. There was a stills session at three thirty. Thank God she didn't have to know any lines for tomorrow. She cursed her stupidity. She should have used the time from Los Angeles to study the new script instead of hitting the champagne. The truth was, she hated the script and wanted no part of the film. Her agent had flown from London to Hollywood to persuade her to accept the deal. He had known why she dreaded it. It was too close to home.

"But use all that emotion, Sophie. Believe me, this film is the best one for you at this stage in your career." She had wanted to be in another film. A comedy set in Mexico. "Darling, they're going for someone a teensy weensy bit younger." That had hurt. She was still only twenty-nine. Was her life to be over by thirty? Was this the time to start the face lifts? And when did the clamps begin? She had heard the screams from one forty-year-old actress as her hair had been twisted at the temples and then clamped under her wig. Sophie dreaded the thought of searching each day for signs of ageing as she had seen others do.

"Believe me Sophie, this is the best offer I can get you at the moment." Jacob was a good agent. He only ever wanted what was best for her. Reluctantly she had agreed to do it. As he had waved goodbye, Jacob had shouted, "Remember Sophie, drag out your screen time."

She found the refrigerated drinks cabinet and helped herself to a vodka and tonic. Outside the rain had stopped and people's voices filtered through the noise of passing cars. She watched them from the window and waited for the anxious loneliness that she always felt in hotel rooms.

After lighting a cigarette, she rummaged through her case for the script. Thumbing the pages, she searched for all the scenes in which she had little or no dialogue. With any luck these would be the first she would have to film. It would give the unknown Seamus Lynch time to perfect her Irish accent.

The film was set in the nineteen-twenties. It was about a family living in Balbriggan, a small coastal town twenty miles north of Dublin. The story began with the General Election and ended at the start of the Civil War.

She found the scene where the Royal Irish Constabulary

came to take away her father. It brought back the pain of childhood. She could hear her own childish screams.

"Leave my Dad alone."

Sophie had stood in a grimy doorway watching while the police had driven him away, arresting him for armed robbery. His had not been a political crime.

She brushed away the tears. When she came to do the scene, she would let the director give her the motivation. There would be more acting off the set than on. After she had finished, the director would praise her intuitive performance. She would congratulate him for his gift for communication. No one would suspect the truth.

She paced the room ramming the words of dialogue into her brain and trying to ignore the hunger gnawing her stomach.

"Watch your weight, Sophie," her agent continually reminded her. "Remember, a moment on the lips, two inches on the hips. I'm sending you more Stoller's pills." Well the effects from the last dose had worn off. If she took any now she would be up all night. The last time she had taken them to get through a night shoot, her chest had become so wheezy that the sound operator had complained.

Her stomach rebelled. She picked up the phone and asked for room service. The decision turned the pancreatic juices into a raging flood. A friendly voice informed her that the chef finished at ten o'clock. She reacted to the news with screams of frustrated abuse. In ten minutes she was dressed and out searching the Dublin streets for a fish and chip shop.

How many times had she played this scene? Sophie stood on O'Connell Bridge and watched the muddy Liffey move sluggishly towards the sea. As she dug her fingers into the hot battered cod and crammed the forbidden calories into her mouth, past conversations with half-known personalities skimmed through her mind. She watched the lights dance through the water and reviewed her celluloid legacy to the British films of the sixties. In two films her scenes had taken place on Vauxhall Bridge. In one film she had been raped as she crossed the bridge and in another she had been pursued across it by something from outer space. On both occasions there had been a moment when she had stood alone, watching the swirling river and waiting for the command "Action".

Now it was the first year into the seventies, she was working for the Americans and the money and hotels were better. A satisfied belch followed the last crumbly mouthful. Feeling like a wild child, she screwed up the paper and let it drop into the murky water. She watched it until it unfolded into a wave.

The fine rain brushed her face and baptised her with freedom. Anonymity and darkness were her chaperones, guarding her from people's nagging demands and expectations. She loved walking the streets at night and never felt frightened. It was in hotel rooms and crowds that loneliness played host to all her fears.

She left the bridge and followed the curving road until she came to Merrion Square. Warm glowing lights beckoned to her through beautiful fanlights and elegant Georgian windows. Drawn curtains revealed either the blue flickering light of a shared television experience or people conversing animatedly with unseen companions.

It was as if all her life she had been passing by the glow and safety of others' reflected lives. Childhood memories crept into her thoughts. Wet streets in Hackney. Rain soaking through her navy school mackintosh as she trudged reluctantly home. The warm lights from neighbours' houses and the coldness within her own home. Which Uncle would be visiting Mum this time?

She shivered and looked around. The rain was now falling

heavily. She increased her pace and dismissed the retrospections. Why ruin an evening with thoughts that should be used for work?

She hurried along Leinster Street until she found Dawson Street. As she approached the hotel, she saw a young couple standing under an umbrella waiting for a taxi. Their arms were entwined and they looked very much in love. Sophie stopped in her tracks and became observer and participator of the moment. If this was a film, she thought, they would be cast with the kind of classical actors who dropped Gielgud anecdotes during coffee breaks, while she would be cast as the waif. Oh boy, did those casting directors know their onions. They were about the same age as herself, in their late twenties, and seemed to carry an air of hope and privilege. She, by contrast, was only a promoted symbol of that same privilege.

A sense of futility overcame her as she went up to her impersonal hotel room. The feeling was followed by its shadow, loneliness. After laying her clothes out neatly for the morning, she escaped from fear with more vodka and the rhythmic monotony of piped hotel music.

Chapter Two

The chauffeur dropped Gloria at the corner of Saint Stephen's Green and Grafton Street.

"I'll pick you up at five o'clock at the Shelbourne, Mrs O'Connell. Are you sure you're all right now?"

"I'm fine Michael. See you later." She watched the chauffeur drive away, then looked to her right and checked the position of the Shelbourne in relation to Grafton Street. She had the whole day to herself and twenty pounds in cash. Enough for a shampoo and set, lunch, and any small purchases. Steve was against her taking a cheque book or credit cards. It was too early to risk temptation. She hovered on the corner, uncertain about what to do. The traffic had been light on the way into Dublin and now she had half an hour to wait before the hairdresser's appointment.

A bus screeched to a halt beside her. Gloria panicked. She experienced the same fear that she had once felt at Grand Central Station. She became confused by the sudden return of memory and wandered distractedly along the pavement trying to hold on to the pictures in her mind. She could see lots of screaming girls with lunchboxes. Of course, she could remember now. Mother was putting her on the train for summer camp. That had been nineteen thirty-six when she had been eight years old. Strange she should remember that year. She could see her mother glancing over her shoulder to the man hovering along the platform. Gloria wasn't supposed to know about him. The boyfriend. She remembered her childish distress. She had always known that her mother didn't like her but on that day she realised that mother also wanted her out of the way. It was then that she'd had the asthma attack on the platform. Gloria heard herself wheezing in sympathy with the child she once was and became aware of the curious looks from people passing her on the pavement.

A stray dog wandered through the traffic and headed into the park. To overcome her acute self-consciousness, Gloria followed.

The dog headed towards a duck pond, part of which was in shadow and covered in thin ice. In the centre of the water, on a rockery, seagulls turned their heads towards the pale morning sun. A pintail duck lifted a webbed foot to scratch his head. Gloria laughed. The bird's movements reminded her of Steve. The dog hurried off past piles of neatly swept leaves with frosted peaks and zigzagged across white covered lawns to a small bridge. Gloria followed and despite the high heeled Charles Jourdan boots was able to keep pace with him.

If she found herself to be stronger it was all due to Steve's efforts. From nineteen forty-four he had served for two years with the army in India and Borneo. When they first met she had hung on to every word about his jungle adventures. And now, from her first waking moment in De Courcy House he had stood like an army captain at the bottom of the bed and announced her fitness schedule.

There had been short walks at first, around the grounds of the house. Then as she became stronger, they had ventured down to the beach, taking the dachshunds with them. The dogs' excitement had made her cry because she remembered the days when they were first married and walking their new puppy, Lottie, through Central Park. Those had been the happy days even though they had been cut off from the family money. Apart from the token gesture of charge accounts at the butcher's and general stores, the only cash available came from Steve's occasional features. She had done her own hair then.

Sounds of gushing water drew her attention to a small waterfall. The stray disappeared into some bushes and began foraging. An old woman called to some seagulls. Taking bread from a shabby shopping bag she threw it to the wheeling birds. Gloria checked her watch. She still had twenty minutes before her appointment. Gingerly, she lowered herself on to a damp, wooden park bench.

Her smart suede pants pinched her crutch. She grappled under her expensive raincoat and adjusted the pressure. Mary's stews were the cause of her discomfort. After a three week diet of stodgy food, even Steve had tired of Mary's "good home cooking". As the housekeeper's feet turned into clay, so Gloria's confidence grew.

She had waited until the woman's day off, then gone to the local butchers to buy some hamburger meat which the Irish called mince. After learning to cope with the strange old-fashioned cooker, she had turned out a pretty good chile con carne. They had eaten it by candle light, sitting in grandeur at each end of the long polished table. The long months of separation had left an awkwardness which had made them strangers but the humour of their situation that evening brought them closer together and the effort at relationship gave way to the old, familiar shorthand. They had made love in front of the log fire and every part of her skin had tingled. Only Steve could make that happen.

Her right leg began to twitch painfully. She eased herself into a standing position and checked her watch. It was only ten minutes before her appointment.

According to Steve, the beauty salon was supposed to be the best one in Dublin. Gloria watched the hairdresser cross the room to talk to some of his regular clients. He had set half her hair, commenting disdainfully on its condition, then left her with the rest of her hair clinging to her neck. She looked at her reflection in the mirror. She appeared and felt as dejected as when she'd been lost on a snipe hunt. It had been hours before they had found her, wandering in the pine forest. Her hair had been soaked by the rain and she'd tripped and lost her glasses. She had been ten. Mother had another lover and sent her off to summer camp again. A tug at her head pulled her back to the present. She told the hairdresser about the tax benefits of moving to Ireland. He became much friendlier and suggested some treatments for her hair. It was always the same, she thought. She, the woman, was always ignored. It was her money that bought friendship.

Under the dryer, she watched some tweed clad women laughing and joking together. Why had she remembered "Camp Happy" today? She rubbed her fingertips against her temples. There was so much missing. So much taken away by the psychiatrists. She'd lost count of all the electroconvulsive therapy treatments. She searched her bruised mind gently, probing backwards in time, feeling the imprints of erased traumas. She had gone for four years, every summer. England was at war when she was twelve. There were a couple of French kids at the camp that year, who told them stories. She tried to remember more but the door to the past had closed.

After coming out of the hairdressers, she browsed awhile round the shops. Then the panic hit her. She regretted looking at the past and was drawn to a pharmacy like a pin to a magnet. The rationalisation began. She needed some make-up, didn't she? Her conscience knew the danger but her legs kept walking towards the red neon sign. Then she saw Sophie.

The young blonde seemed to be sampling every perfume in the shop. There were groans of pleasure as she savoured the scents from each bottle. Gloria hovered in the shop doorway, enjoying Sophie's sensual rapture.

"Hi," she whispered.

Sophie spun round, her eyes sparkling as she sniffed her overscented arm.

"Hi," she replied.

She looked hard at the thin woman with over-bleached hair and dark glasses. Her mackintosh was too long for her and her lipstick had shot over the edge of her lipline. She knew her from somewhere but she wasn't quite sure where. She turned back to the assistant.

"What's the most expensive one? I've got my expenses and I feel wild."

"Joy. It's supposed to really drive men mad."

"Great, let's try it then."

The assistant sprayed her other wrist.

"God that's wonderful. Oh, God, isn't it wonderful?"

Sophie turned to Gloria and waved the wrist under her nose.

"It's a great perfume," Gloria agreed.

"And she's right, it does drive guys wild."

Sophie made up her mind immediately. She would take both the perfume and the cologne. To hell with the expense. Gloria grinned as she shared Sophie's extravagant moment.

"Where do I know you from? Didn't we work together one summer?"

"God no. We saw each other at the airport, four weeks ago. The TWA flight."

"Hell, I was bombed out of my skull, no wonder I couldn't remember."

"Can I get you something, madam?"

The assistant was looking at her curiously. Gloria suddenly felt stupid.

"Oh, just some cottonwool balls."

She fumbled in her bag. Sophie felt a sudden compassion for the strange woman who was scattering Gauloises and tissues everywhere in an attempt to pay quickly.

"Are you doing anything for lunch?" she asked.

"Er, no, I've got till five."

"Well, it's my first day let loose from the mohair suit brigade, and I've got my expenses, so I'll treat you to lunch."

"Great."

Two complete nuts, the chemist's assistant thought, as she watched the pair walk down Grafton Street.

The walls in the hamburger place were covered in psychedelic colours. A recording of the musical *Hair* was playing at full volume, forcing the customers to shout. With her bad eyesight and dark glasses, Gloria managed to crash into every chair en route to the table.

They ordered giant burgers from a lithe youth whose T-shirt didn't quite cover his navel.

"Red wine O.K. for you?" Sophie bawled across the table.

Gloria gripped the edge of the chair tightly. Here was the first test.

"Coke," she gasped.

"What, Cola?" Sophie sounded surprised.

Gloria felt as if brutal hands were squeezing her throat. She took a deep breath and nodded her head.

"Just Coke."

"A carafe of red and a large Coke for my friend."

Gloria lit a Gauloise. Her hands were shaking. Sophie's attention was on the nubile waiter, weaving his way across the restaurant. His hips were swaying in time to the music.

"What do you think?" Sophie asked her. "Is he Arthur or Martha?"

Relief flooded through Gloria's body. A laugh rumbled through her thin frame and challenged the stereophonic sound.

"Don't waste yer perfume on it."

Gloria couldn't remember a time when she'd had so much fun. Sophie's non-stop chatter fanned a growing feeling of warmth and confidence. She was alive again. Not even the deep red colour of Sophie's wine disturbed her. The girl was actually enjoying her company. She knew nothing about her except what she, Gloria, had told her. That she had moved to Dublin because she couldn't bear to live in America any more. Sophie had sympathised with the decision, confiding that she too had been unhappy in Hollywood.

After lunch they explored Brown Thomas and tried on an assortment of hats and Arran sweaters until they were helpless with giggling. The shop assistants recognised Sophie, so tolerated her eccentric behaviour. Gloria, dropping cigarette ash everywhere, was watched suspiciously.

Their madness continued into Duke Street, where they found a small jewellers displaying all the astrological signs.

"What sign are you?" Sophie asked.

"Pisces."

"No, really? So am I."

"You don't say."

"Well, I was born on the nineteenth of February at midnight. So I suppose I could be either Pisces or Aquarius. I think I feel like a Pisces though. When's yours?"

"March the thirteenth. My husband's Pisces too. March the third."

"Oh God, mine was Pisces."

"What?"

"I left him after three weeks. I think we're supposed to marry Scorpios. Does your marriage work?"

"Oh yes." Gloria became loyal. "I don't know what I'd do without Steve."

A cloud of guilt crept into her thoughts. Her day's

happiness had not included Steve. It went when Sophie pulled her into the shop.

The young actress bought two silver fish, one for herself and one for Gloria, then proudly sporting their signs of identity around their necks, they made for Bewleys.

A neatly dressed waitress laid out some cakes and a pot of tea. Gloria looked around the large crowded tearooms. There was old polished wood everywhere. It made her think of her grandfather, in his study, sitting reading the *New York Times*.

"I've got to leave in half an hour," Sophie announced. "I've got to meet an estate agent. There's a cottage I might rent in Ballsbridge. I'm so sick of being cooped up in hotels."

"I hate hotels too," Gloria murmured then lapsed into silence.

Sophie attacked a cream cake. Tomorrow she would have to increase the Stoller's pills but today she was going to indulge.

"Tom was a Scorpio." Gloria sounded mournful.

"What?" Sophie's mouth was full of cake.

"My first husband."

Gloria stared vacantly into space. Her dark glasses reflected the daylight from the café windows.

"He jumped out of a window on the sixty-fourth floor."

Sophie choked on her cake.

"You'd better stick to Pisceans."

Gloria's sad memory disappeared. "Hah, so much for the goddam zodiac."

She let out a laugh that shattered the tearoom. The people at the neighbouring table, already overcome by the Gauloise smoke, took it as their cue to vacate their seats. Sophie chuckled. Gloria was the ultimate deterrent, guaranteed to clear any space around them.

"I've got to run." Sophie settled the bill and gathered up her belongings. Gloria watched her furry outline wistfully.

"Let's keep in touch, shall we?"

"Okay. What's your phone number?"

Sophie took a biro and held out the back of a cigarette packet waiting for a reply. Gloria racked her brains. It was no use. She couldn't remember her own number.

"Aw, hell, I don't know it."

She felt inadequate.

"Well, you can get me at the Hibernian or at Ardmore studios. See you."

Gloria felt as if the party had moved to someone else's house. She waited for the usual self-consciousness but it didn't arrive. Instead she found herself casually looking at her watch to check the time. She breathed in deeply and didn't cough. She was calm for the first time in years.

She approached the Shelbourne with a new sense of pride. She had survived the whole day, made a friend and had a ball. She couldn't wait to see Steve's face when he was told that she still had fifteen pounds change. The Mercedes slid into the kerb and Gloria stepped into the plush comfort smiling like the Mona Lisa.

"Did you have a good time then, Mrs O'Connell?"

The chauffeur looked at her cautiously.

"I sure did."

They drove past women laden with shopping.

"Where's Ballsbridge, Michael?" she asked.

"We're just coming into it after this bridge, Mrs O'Connell."

Clusters of school children were queuing for buses. Their shouts and laughter cut through the noise of the traffic. Gloria fingered the silver Pisces symbol and smiled contentedly. She had a friend. Someone who actually liked her for herself. Not since that first week at "Camp Happy", when she had found a pal, had she felt so complete. What was the kid's name? Her mind searched through the splinters of the past. Images of camp fires and the smells of night air returned. More fragments of memory. She remembered a shared birthday cake at boarding school. What was her name? Gloria couldn't remember the girl's name.

A motor horn was tapped outside. The rhythm vibrated through Gloria's subconscious.

"Boop boop dit-em dot-em what-em Chu," she shouted.

"Pardon, Mrs O'Connell?"

Gloria sang lustily.

"What's that song, Mrs O'Connell?"

"Aw, it was my favourite song as a kid, about some little fish."

"Now you mention, I have heard it."

Gloria patiently taught him the words, laughing as he fumbled with the dot-ems and what-ems. By the time they reached De Courcy House, she was as high as a skunk.

*

"There's a Russian Orthodox priest in exile on one side and the Dublin Communist Party on the other. So you won't be bored, will you?" The estate agent laughed, showing nicotine-stained teeth. They were perfect accessories to his whole brown, tweedy appearance, Sophie thought. She crinkled her eyes and attempted to smile. Having agreed to take the cottage for two months, all she needed now were the lease and keys. But he wanted to chat. He thrust his hands into his pockets and aimed a tan-coloured shoe at a stray twig. He was fair haired, in his mid-thirties and had managed to inform her between the bedroom and bathroom that his name was Patrick, that he was single and that in Ireland, they took their time to find the right girl. He complained that it was hard to find a broad-minded girl in Dublin. He used the same whining tone as her father when he returned to jail for the second time. "What chance did I have, Sophie?" He even looked like him.

"There's a good delicatessen around the corner from here. I don't suppose you film people get much time for cooking, do you?"

Sophie assured him that she hated cooking, all housework and was devoted to her career. He tried to make his expression one of understanding but it crept into a leer. He started to tell her about his friends at the Abbey Theatre. Sophie wanted to end the conversation. She felt uneasy with Dublin men. Repressed sex hung in the air. The little waiter who regularly brought brandy to her room had one night thrown himself at her knees and asked whether she could sell him some Durex. She being a person in fillums, he had babbled, must have access to such things. She had bitterly and drunkenly explained that she of all people was least able to give him help. She had then treated him to a story about her own life. A maudlin habit developed in the last six months. A succession of waiters and cloakroom attendants had been subjected to her slurred confessions. Cringing with embarrassment he had left the room whispering his apologies.

The next day, full of remorse for her behaviour, she had approached the sound operator and told him the story. He was glad to offload his supply.

"You're doing me a favour girl," he joked.

"The wife's arriving tomorrow, and she's only got the loop, hasn't she."

That evening she had seen the waiter hovering around the cloakroom and given him the forbidden package. Since then, he hadn't been on night duty.

"Would you like me to give you a lift to your hotel?" The estate agent looked hopeful.

"No, it's not far, I'll walk it. Give me a chance to explore."

"I'll probably see you again soon."

"It's a small world."

"It is that."

"Well, don't let me keep you."

She turned her back on him and took a last look at the cottage. Weeds dotted the small courtyard. Not even the freshly painted door could disguise the shabbiness of the place. The "bijoux cottage" even had grass growing out of the guttering. Sophie felt uneasy. Why had she picked a mews? Why not a flat? Was she trying to reproduce the neat mews cottage off Seymour Place? The home she had shared with David?

Dusk was settling and the priest inside the adjoining cottage switched on a porch light. Sophie felt alone and lost. She hated the feeling. Was it retribution for joking with the American woman about the marriage?

She hurried along the lane. The muffled noise from the traffic on Pembroke Road which ran parallel to the mews reminded her of the sound of the Park Lane traffic which she often heard from Jacob's flat in Mayfair. Distraught and tearful, it was to Jacob, her friend and agent, that she had turned, when one day, after coming home early from filming, she'd found her husband, David, in bed with another actor, a man she knew quite well. Jacob and his friend Henry had consoled her.

"I tried to warn you dear." Jacob had held her tightly, his scented softness absorbing her pain.

"He's always been that way, Sophie," Henry had said. "He should have told you, the selfish boy."

They had cosseted her. Taken her to plays and parties, where she gaily announced that David hadn't liked her cooking. Smile Sophie, she had been told, make light of it Sophie. She had behaved well. Not one gossip columnist had found out the real story. Soon the scandal of the three week marriage was yesterday's news. David continued to play romantic leads and his fans were never disillusioned.

She reached the end of the lane and turned right towards the main road. A gust of cold wind sighed round her shoulders bringing tears which helped her anxiety and self-pity. She blamed the company accountant for her decision to rent the cottage. He had refused to pay for her nocturnal bouts.

"The contract definitely states that we are responsible for all your food and laundry but not your bar bills." He had tried to reason with her but she had reacted impulsively.

"Okay give me my expenses and I'll look after myself. I hate hotels . . ."

The road to hell is signposted with grand gestures, she thought bitterly. She'd blown some of the expenses today, so she would have to ask for a month in advance to keep the estate agent happy.

A shower of rain now joined the cold wind, so that the delicatessen appeared like a beacon in the gloom. She peered through the window. It was a well stocked store with rows of wines and spirits. She decided to introduce herself and buy a bottle of brandy.

"Can you spare some money for the baby?"

The dirty red face belonged to a woman. Sophie reeled from her sudden appearance. Her eyes focused on the ragged bundle in the tinker woman's arms. Grey mucus dribbled from the baby's nose. The pair were often seen touting outside the hotel. Sophie fumbled for her purse while racking her memory for lost time.

"Bless ye kind lady."

The tinker scurried off in the direction of some Americans.

The receptionist shouted to her as she entered the hotel lobby.

"Oh, Miss Smith, your producer, Mr Shapiro, was enquiring about you. The chauffeur waited for over an hour."

She handed her a key with a message attached. Sophie leant against the desk, breathing heavily.

"Something about, yes, they were expecting you at a soirée."

Alarm bells rang in Sophie's head.

"Shit, the bloody party. What's the time?"

The receptionist looked ruffled.

"It's nine o'clock," she said slowly and precisely.

Sophie rushed to the lift.

The only way she could get into the evening dress was to lie on the bed and pull it on. Her body was clammy with fear. What had happened to the time? She hurriedly patched her make-up, searching her face for an answer. She couldn't find her own self in the mirror; a stranger's eyes returned her look. The secret was locked in another part of her mind. It was revealed as her taxi drove past a pub. The lights brought back her memory. When she had left the delicatessen and started walking towards the hotel, the rain had turned to sleet. She had heard the ballad singers as she walked past the pub. The lights had been so welcoming and the singers so young and boisterous that she had shared the brandy with them. Then there was blackness. Her chest became a network of icy nerves.

"Sophie, what kept you?"

Paul Shapiro looked at her anxiously.

Sophie spoke clearly and carefully.

"I'm sorry Paul. I couldn't find your number."

Her eyes were wide and childish.

"I ran into some old friends in the country and there were all these sheep . . ."

She waved her arms vaguely.

"Oh, this really is a beautiful house, Paul."

Stoller's pills were working. Her eyes felt stretched to the back of her skull.

"When you're not sure of a word, Sophie, don't use it."
How many times had Jacob told her to think carefully before
she spoke. Well, now she was thinking. She was introduced to
the other guests. A floating, smiling enigma.

"I'm Melvyn Hughes. I'm with Metropolitan Films."

Sophie balanced the plate of food carefully before looking
up into keen, alert blue eyes. He was dressed in a well-cut
safari-style suit. Brown curls framed a smooth, handsome
face.

"May I sit with you?"

"Help yourself."

She tried to manoeuvre a thread of chicken from her teeth.

"I've been watching rushes today. You're quite
wonderful."

"Mmm."

The piece of chicken was proving awkward.

"I can't think of anyone else who could give the part so
much . . ." He paused, his hands in a praying position.
"Soul."

"Oh, thanks."

The tips of the praying hands were moving sensuously
across his lips. Sophie was fascinated. The chicken became
dislodged.

"You're going to collect all the awards for this."

"Do you really think so?"

He continued with more lavish praise and Sophie soaked it
up gratefully. He told her that, really, he was an academic
who had been caught up in the strange world of films by
mistake, that he was over in Ireland to visit an author about
writing a screenplay and just by chance had met Paul and
been invited up to the studios and then on to the party. He
talked about the social significance of *Daughters of Destiny*
and how the problems in the North were getting worse.

Sophie was attentive. Her own education being limited, she

35

was always overawed by academics. It was Jacob who had furthered her education by introducing her to literature.

"Stretch your mind ducky. Sophie, in this business, it pays to be middle-class. Improve yourself, my dear. All of us who come out of the East End have to work that bit harder than everyone else."

It was Henry who worked on her accent. He had been an actor in Harry Hanson's repertory company before giving up the business to keep house for Jacob.

"Bright-eyed Ida, riding on a bicycle. Little brother Isaac riding on a tricycle. Red leather, yellow leather. I won't tell you how to act Sophie because you're a natural. All I am dear, is a bundle of tricks and bad habits."

Melvyn Hughes appeared to be genuinely interested in her thoughts, her motivations and about her intuitive feelings for the film. He chose his words carefully and fetched her brandies although he hardly seemed to drink anything himself. She felt caught on a cloud of wonderful empathy.

It was the lessons learnt in the street of hard knocks that were responsible for the warning signals. The lone, alley cat instincts reached up to her lofty, euphoric state when he casually asked what she was being paid for playing Kate.

"Whatever you do Sophie, don't let anyone know that I've agreed a special low for *Daughters of Destiny*."

Jacob's voice echoed in her ear.

"This is an investment for much bigger deals in the future." The money for her next film was being negotiated at that moment and Melvyn Hughes' company had a share in the production.

"Piss off," she said.

She needed air and space. She let herself out through a small glass door leading to the gardens. Oblivious of the wet grass, she wandered towards an old oak tree. The sky had cleared to reveal a full moon surrounded by a misty halo.

Hitching her skirt, she began to climb the tree. She found a comfortable position in the twisting trunk and listened to the droning of a distant plane. A part of her was dying. She was playing the wrong part in the wrong story and she wanted out. She lifted her face to the moon's rays. The tears were cold by the time they reached her chin. She tried awkwardly to suck her thumb. Anything to escape the aching loneliness.

"Help me," she whispered to the moon. "I'm drowning."

Chapter Three

Gloria's brief happiness ended abruptly.

"Okay Mouse. Where did you get them?"

When she described her day to Steve he'd looked disappointed. It was almost as if he'd expected her to fail. During supper he had behaved like an aloof stranger and it occurred to her that although he wanted her to get stronger, he was frightened of losing her dependence. She couldn't cope with the thought. Rather than confronting him with her anger, she turned it back on herself, choking and spilling her coffee. She fled upstairs to the dogs. Their soft warm bodies calmed her and she wondered why it was that only animals had ever given her unconditional love. In bed, he had ignored her "let's make up" mouse noises and turned his back. She lay fingering the Pisces symbol, the memory of the outing with Sophie reawakening her spirit of rebellion.

The following day, Steve announced that Rachel was coming for dinner on the nineteenth.

"Don't I have any say about who comes here?" she had shouted. "Jesus Christ, my money pays for all this."

She knew she had broken the cardinal rule and violated the covenant between them. The greyness and sadness in his face brought back all her guilt and self-loathing. Frightened of being left alone, the rebel gave up her freedom to become a mouse again, protected by his arms and cuddled into the warmth of his neck.

Mist was swirling across the lawn. Gloria stood by the window and listened to the rhythmic, flat wails from the foghorn. The sound was like a part of herself trying to be heard. Something fluttered across the grass. It looked like a snipe. She felt a call from the past which became more intense. It brought a longing for the smell of blueberries ripening in the sun or the smell of toasted marshmallows from a camp fire. She wanted to hear the sound of twigs snapping in a pine forest. She searched for a name, a glimpse of the hidden being that was locked in her mind.

Steve was fumbling in his pocket for a tissue. He produced a pathetic grey scrap and searched for a clean corner.

"Steve."

"Yep."

"Why don't you get Rachel to bring Sophie on Thursday?"

"Could you handle it?"

"Sure."

She lit a Gauloise and planned what to wear. She would make sure that Sophie had a wonderful evening and then there would be a surprise . . . She drifted into a daydream.

"Mouse, come back."

"Wa . . ."

"You're sure you can cope?"

"Please Steve."

She buried her nose into his hair and scratched his temples.

"All right Mouse. We'll see what we can do."

*

Sophie attempted to look at her reflection in the mirror but jelly-like cells danced in her vision. Her eyes were puffy from the previous night's binge and her shoulders ached from falling over the chair on the way to bed. She could hear the shouts outside from the riggers carrying the scaffolding towards the tumbledown cottage and the yells from the sparks adjusting the lamps. The calor gas fumes hurt her chest so she wrapped an Arran cardigan round her shoulders and opened the caravan door. The cold damp air cleared her eyes. A light mist hovered over the caravans. The sound of the nine o'clock news came from the make-up van where Bill and his assistants were seeing to the extras. Bill was a gentle giant of a man who looked more like a lumberjack than a patient moulder of faces. Next to him were Gladys and Clara, the hairdressers. They were round, cosy women whose caravan was the Clapham Junction of all company scandal and gossip. Sophie watched a wardrobe assistant dart across the field towards the caterer's van where some assistants were eating bacon butties. She wished she could grow wings and fly away. The whole unit was moving relentlessly towards the scene that she dreaded. She felt the familiar nausea.

Sophie Rainbow had watched her father being arrested twice. The first time had been when she was seven years old. She'd had nightmares for years reliving the experience of seeing her father struggling with the police as they took him away. It had been night time. She had tried to fight them off until her mother had pulled her away. He had disappeared out of her world and returned seven years later as a thin stranger who found it difficult to speak to her. Two years later he was arrested again for breaking parole. He'd robbed a cinema. This time she had felt acute shame. She had been returning home for tea with a new boyfriend when she had seen them pushing him into the car. Dad went back to Dartmoor and she never saw the boyfriend again. When she confided in Jacob, he suggested that she change her name to Smith.

"Let's keep stumm about all that dear. Just in case. People can be very cruel, especially if you're successful. I remember buying my first really good suit. My mother was so proud. As I was walking down the street, someone I'd known from the neighbourhood called me a dirty kike. Envy Sophie. People hate you to be successful and if you aim for the stars, there's a lot of them ready to shoot you down."

Henry had echoed his sentiments. "I understudied Jack Buchanan. Well, I understudied his understudy and I went on one Wednesday matinée. You have never heard such bitching. Yet they all loved me when I just had 'Dinner is served, Sir' to say."

"Have you had your breakfast Sophie?"

Moira, her stand-in, climbed the caravan steps and caught sight of a cigarette end sticking out of Sophie's congealed bacon buttie.

"Do you still feel bad then?" she asked.

"My nerve ends are hanging out of the ends of my fingers and my bum is trying to reach my belly button. Apart from that I'm great."

Moira looked over her shoulder cautiously.

"Would the hair of the dog help?"

"What have you got there?"

The stand-in giggled and pulled a baby's hot water bottle out of her basket.

"It's to warm my hands. It'll see you through the scene but don't let on it was me gave it to you, you promise now."

Sophie promised. Shouts for Moira echoed across the field. "I'd better get back." She gathered up her belongings.

"Don't worry about the eyes Sophie, they're lighting full on you."

Sophie watched her trudging through the mud towards the shouting cameramen. To drink or not to drink. She took hold of the water bottle. It would be breaking her first commandment. Thou shalt not drink upon the set. She had worked with the wrecks who needed it first thing in the morning. It was the one rule that she had kept when bombing out. Never

41

at work. She poured out the pale, golden liquid. Just this once. This was a special scene, she rationalised. All the emotional landmarks in her life had to be used this morning. After today, she would never whore them again.

The Black and Tans were grappling with the desperate looking Irishman.

"Oi'll be back," he shouted to Sophie who was being held back by some women extras.

The hot, dark, internal tears dribbled out on cue, staining her carefully shaded, rosy cheeks.

"Look after your mother, Katy."

The actor was being led away, still struggling.

The soul that revealed itself to no human emerged for the camera. In a minute all misery and pain from childhood was recorded.

"Da . . ." she screamed.

The eerie child's wail rang across the muddy field. Watching onlookers were transfixed by the anguished cry.

"CUT."

"Daddy wouldn't buy me a bow wow."

It was her truth that had created the atmosphere of reverent silence. Now it was her right to destroy it. She delighted in the shocked look on the crew's faces. They had answered her performance with sympathy, now she wanted the confessional burnt to the ground. They had seen her commune with her own soul, now she gave them the golden calf of disillusion, her daily experience.

She brushed away the tears as if they were obsolete props.

"Print?" she asked the director.

"It's a print, Sophie."

He knew how to handle her in this mood. He turned some pages of the script before meeting her suspicious look head on.

"Good girl." He smiled. "You've got a change for the next scene, haven't you?"

Sophie appeared satisfied. She made her way across the field to the caravan, the effort of negotiating the mud distracting her from her soiled emotions. Jacob's phone call the previous night had guaranteed a fresh impetus for her creative work. Bill Rainbow, her jailbird father, was coming out in June. "Sophie's new release," she muttered bitterly to herself.

Dad was fifty-three now. He'd lost his thirties and forties to Her Majesty and his wife, Maggie, to Percy, a Fulham hairdresser. God, how she hated her family. Scumbags the lot of them.

She reached the top of the caravan steps and turned back to watch the men rehearsing a fight. The fight arranger's high-pitched voice was muffled by the damp air. She thought of the earnest, socialist writers she had met, who extolled the virtue of the working classes. She laughed out loud thinking of the scenes where warm-hearted women laid clean kitchen tables, while their husbands discussed subjects of deep social significance. The reality of living on the bent, wrong side of the tracks, was beyond their sensitive imaginations. On that side were greed, pettiness and the preoccupation with trivia. As a child, she had often wondered whether she was adopted. She couldn't fit in. Enid Blyton—a whole world of different values available at the local library—hadn't helped. Miss Warner, the enlightened teacher who smelt of lavender and wore grey, pencil skirts, had fed the urgent need to escape.

"Sophie, people, no matter what their backgrounds, can always change their lives. All it takes is effort."

Sophie made the effort and moved out of Hackney into a small bedsitter in Belsize Park. Maggie Rainbow had been relieved. She had decided to change her status to that

43

of Percy's mistress. She came off National Assistance, moved to Fulham and used mayonnaise instead of salad cream.

Sophie found work in a Soho coffee bar where a whole new world of actors, debutantes and students, inspired her. She would listen discreetly to their conversations, then later, in the privacy of the bedsitter, assume their voices and copy their mannerisms. Then she won "Miss West End" in a competition at the Lyceum. The prize was one thousand pounds, a new wardrobe of clothes, and a film test. She had called herself Sophie Russell, taking the name of the man they continually discussed in the coffee bar. Jacob had been one of the judges. He had given her his card. It was a week before she visited his office, fearing that he might be just a dirty old man. Jacob had shown her how to use a knife and fork properly, stood by while she made her film test, lovingly groomed her career and given her a childhood. Henry and Jacob took a surrogate daughter and gave her the Christmases and birthdays Sophie had never known. Maggie's crude explicit attitude to life had made the girl old by nine. She had been treated as an adult sounding board for Maggie's insecurities and grievances. Jacob and Henry helped her to find magic, experience irresponsibility and never intruded on her independent spirit.

"Sophie."

Rachel Myers, dressed from head to toe in Arran, strode across the field towards her.

"Sophie," she paused for breath. "We've been invited to dinner at the O'Connells."

"Oh yes, and who the hell are the O'Connells?"

The large woman sighed with frustration.

"Steve said you and Gloria knew each other. You had lunch in Dublin together or something."

Rachel looked at Sophie warily. "Are you free on Thursday night? I've got to ring them back."

"Gloria?"

Rachel began to lose patience.

"The American woman, blonde, you had lunch with her."

Sophie remembered dark glasses and madness.

"Oh, her, I like her, yeah sure, what time?"

Rachel spoke slowly and firmly. "Seven-thirty. I'll collect you in the car. Put something warm on. I don't think they've got central heating."

She headed towards some refined English voices. They were the knights booked to play the grand, historical parts. Sophisticated West End actresses were there to play their wives.

"Sophie, when you've changed, come for a check, I need to look at your eyes."

"Sophie, when you've been to Bill, I need to check your hair."

"She won't be long."

Her dresser joined in the rallying call.

Sophie climbed into the caravan and grabbed the baby's hot water bottle.

It was Thursday, the nineteenth of February. Gloria watched the last rays from the sun straining through the mist. The persistent stream of light promised the rebirth of spring. She turned back to the mirror and checked her make-up. From downstairs came the sounds of pans clattering and raised voices. Gloria smiled wickedly. Steve had found another woman to do the cooking and Mary was assisting. Holy Mary, scourge of the confessional, she went at least three times a week, was having to put humility into practice. Maureen was younger, more efficient, highly recommended and more expensive. Steve's tactful way of breaking the news

45

to the older woman that she was to work from nine to four when Maureen would take over, was to appear concerned that she spent more time with her family. Maureen had made the birthday cake in the shape of a fish and covered it in soft, white icing. Gloria touched her Pisces symbol and chuckled in anticipation of Sophie's surprised expression. Outside the mist was clearing, enabling her to see the lights from a dinghy in the bay. The sight of it bobbing on the water brought another memory of lights and shapes from somewhere in the past. She closed her eyes and attempted to find the source of the image but it eluded her like so many of her thoughts.

*

Sophie rummaged through the dirty basket until she found a pair of unladdered tights. After rinsing them through quickly, she dried them with her hairdryer. It was nearly seven o'clock and Rachel would inevitably be on time. The loud voice had shouted a reminder just as she was finishing a scene. Sophie hadn't for once lingered in the bar but had made straight for the cottage feeling guilty for forgetting. She took a sober look at the cottage and made some resolutions. It really was time that she got to grips with herself. She decided that she would find a launderette and clean up the place. It was beginning to look like a tip. There were unwashed dishes in the kitchen sink. The lounge smelt of stale tobacco and booze. Everywhere were signs of her chaotic existence. She knew that really she should have stayed in the hotel but her pride forced her to persevere with the outward sign of independence.

The elastic was passably dry just as the doorbell rang. Sophie yanked on the tights and hastily checked her appearance. She had lost more weight. The green, Donald Davis dress, hung on her. She wished that her face wasn't so puffed.

Rachel entered like a grotesque Red Riding Hood in a red kaftan and matching cape.

"How do you like it?" she said proudly, swirling round for Sophie's approval.

"Incredible. Where did you get it?"

"There's a little boutique in Dalkey run by a French woman."

She lifted her skirts.

"Look."

Sophie saw red stockinged feet squeezed into red patent pumps.

"Incredible."

"Are you ready?"

Sophie grabbed her silver fox and hurried Rachel out before she lost interest in herself and took in the chaos of the lounge.

There was an overpowering smell of Joy and cigarette smoke in the car. Even the driver kept his window open. When they arrived at Black Rock, Rachel leapt out and breathed in the sea air. Steve hurried to meet them and helped Sophie struggle from the back seat.

"Hi Sophie, I'm Steve. Glad you could make it."

Gloria, dressed in a tight-fitting, silver trouser-suit, stood in the doorway. Her silver-blonde hair was lacquered into a large chignon and large silver sunglasses covered half her face. A Gauloise protruded from a long silver cigarette holder.

"Hi," she croaked.

Sophie began to laugh.

"What's funny?" Gloria said.

"You look like the tin man in the Wizard of Oz."

"What?"

The penny slowly dropped. Instead of being offended Gloria roared with laughter. Rachel's shocked expression started Sophie off with more giggling until Steve took charge and ushered them all into the house.

"Come on now, girls."

Rachel was bewildered as the spontaneous madness continued. Steve too, watched the great rapport between the two women. It was most unusual for Gloria to react so easily with another female. Something disturbed him. It was almost as if she'd been on the pills.

Not until the laughter subsided was Sophie able to take in the enormous hallway and sweeping staircase. None of this splendour went with the image she had of the sad-faced little woman whom she had first seen in Grafton Street.

"But I thought you were hard up."

Gloria's shrewd eyes watched the young actress' embarrassed confusion.

"Only in the think box," she replied.

She took Sophie's arm and led her into the lounge.

Rachel showed familiarity by announcing to Sophie that Gloria was a Van Heerden.

"A what?"

"It just means my family is rich. That's my problem."

Gloria dismissed the subject, took Sophie's fur coat and casually threw it over the back of a chair. Steve registered Sophie's concern for the coat. He picked it up gently and called Mary for a hanger. Sophie was grateful. She listened to Rachel gushing about the house and dropping the names of knights appearing in the film. They had to be really rich for that one to be so effusive. She felt let down, the same feeling she had experienced when she was twelve and the girl in her class at Cassland Road School had invited her to a birthday party. Maggie had given her a face flannel and soap in a brown paper bag to give as a present. She had set off happily from her home in Wall Street to the address in Victoria Park Road. The front of the house had been different from her area and the people had been smartly dressed. That hadn't worried her. It was when she realised that everyone else had given

48

presents in pretty wrapping paper that she became aware of
the social difference. It hadn't been spam and egg sandwiches
but a sit-down supper. There had been the question "What
does your father do?" The dry throat and quick invention,
then panic when she realised that they ate bread with their left
hand and she used her right.

"What will you drink, Sophie?"

"Vodka and tonic."

"You, Rachel?"

"Oh, I'll just have some wine."

Sophie watched Steve pour the drinks. He seemed a quiet
type of man. He and Gloria were like a well-oiled double act.
She would make an entertaining statement and he would
reply with a "Yes dear" or "That's right dear". Gloria with
Steve at her side was far more extrovert than she had been on
her own in Dublin. Steve handed her an orange juice.

"Aren't you having a drink, Gloria?" Sophie asked.

The American woman fingered her neck as if searching for
something.

"No."

She lit another Gauloise, although one was already burning in the ashtray. Sophie was puzzled by the woman's return
to timidity.

Gloria didn't want to make excuses to Sophie, she wanted
her to understand. She looked to Steve for approval. He
nodded reassuringly. She took a deep breath.

"I'm an alcoholic."

"A what?"

"Gloria's an alcoholic, dear." Steve spelt out the words.
"She mustn't drink alcohol."

"What, not even one?"

Sophie was horrified.

"Not even one."

Steve was emphatic.

49

Out of the corner of her eye, Sophie could see Red Riding Hood looking like she'd just seen her Grandma raped by the wolf. She began to laugh.

"Blimey, what happens if you do?"

Gloria grinned at her.

"I guess I'd behave pretty badly."

Her eyes glinted with past memories.

"And she'd end up in hospital in a padded room," Steve snapped.

The glint in Gloria's eyes was shaded by a meekness, she appeared to shrink into the chair. Sophie, silenced by Steve, became aware of the dampness in her tights' elastic and the sound of her own swallowing.

Rachel launched into reminiscences about Hollywood days, Steve gratefully accepted the change in subject. Gloria felt desperate. The evening wasn't supposed to go badly like this.

"Look Sophie." She pointed to the little Pisces sign worn at her neck.

"I've got my fish."

Sophie stared at the funny, rich woman who had actually treasured the trinket given in a spontaneous gesture of friendship. She held her own fish in the light.

"I've got mine too."

They sat grinning at each other, recapturing the madness of their first meeting.

"I'm a Pisces."

Rachel butted into their sanctum of craziness.

"But I think a lot of it's cancelled out by my moon in Virgo."

"You make it sound like a disease," Sophie yelled, the vodka warming her up. Steve's voice purred through the women's high pitched discussion.

"Well girls, that makes four of us."

Gloria relaxed. Everyone had some theory on astrology no matter how banal. Even Rachel began to let herself go and allow the vowels to slip occasionally. Sophie had warmed to the mood and Steve began recounting juicy gossip from Hollywood days using astrology as his central theme. Gloria had heard all the stories before but she enjoyed listening to the different permutations over the years. Some of them were from old Reader's Digests but Steve sounded so authoritative that by all accounts even she would swear that he had taken part in the happenings.

Unlike Mary, who crashed about the house, Maureen crept, seeming to materialise into rooms. She announced that dinner was ready so discreetly that the transference of the four talking people from around the blazing log fire in the lounge into the long polished dining room was accomplished with the minimum amount of effort.

At each end of the dining room was a roaring log fire. The flames threw dancing shadows on the high, beamed ceiling. Large windows, overlooking the bay, reflected the flickering lights from the tall candles in the centre of the table.

"Oh," Sophie gasped.

She was used to the open log fires in California, the fake fires on film sets and the spluttering gas fires in London, but she had never been in a palatial home with two fireplaces in one large room before. She felt an immediate reverence for this cathedral of warmth.

"Get a load of this."

"What a beautiful room, Steve."

Rachel remained poised. "I haven't seen a room like this since I stayed in a castle in Scotland."

"Were you on a film at the time?" Sophie asked.

Reluctantly, Rachel admitted that she had been.

Gloria blew her nose and threw the tissue into the fire.

51

"Kevin O'Higgins died here. Right across this table," she announced.

"Oh," Rachel said. "I thought he died in Boothestown."

"No, we were told that some guy shot him outside here on the way to mass and he managed to stagger into this house before he died."

Rachel was fascinated by the story and told them which knight was playing the part of the famous Minister of Justice in *Daughters of Destiny*. She and Sophie sat diagonally opposite each other at the table, while Steve and Gloria presided from each end. Sophie began to giggle. Gloria had a plastic rose by her side and when she pressed it, Maureen popped out of the kitchen. Sophie bent down to look under the table; a wire trailed across the room and lying over a part of it was one of the dachshunds.

To counteract Sophie's behaviour Rachel became formal, straightening her back and eating her food delicately while introducing the subject of the dollar deficit. Gloria, immediately on her home territory of finance, advised Rachel to invest in gold. Sophie was in a haze of euphoria from the effects of the vodka, wine and hot food. She felt at ease with these people, who were now discussing the international monetary fund. Gloria talked easily about her money without any coyness. Sophie came to the conclusion that although Gloria, on paper, was worth about a million, she had no real control of her money. It was tied up in trust funds and controlled by banks and lawyers. There seemed to be a continual battle for an increase in income. She felt sorry for the American woman. At least when she earned her money, it was hers to blow or do with as she pleased.

Gloria, deep in conversation, pressed the rose unintentionally and Maureen leapt through the kitchen door. There was a pause while Gloria looked up. They were only half way through the pudding.

"A box of tissues, Maureen, please."

Sophie nearly wet herself. This started Gloria off and all discussions over finance came to an end. Rachel fuelled the new, bawdy atmosphere with gossip about the actors on the film set. She went into lengthy descriptions of their reputations and recounted past scandals. Sophie was intrigued, the stories being completely new to her. She learnt that the actor playing her father, who she had noticed was a little bow legged for the past week, had recently had a vasectomy, unknown to his mistress who was hoping to get pregnant. One of the West End actresses, who walked around being unbearably refined had the reputation of being able to shoot Pears soap out of her vagina, whilst submerged in a bath, with such force that it could hit the ceiling. Sophie was amazed that a whole sub-culture was going on of which she was entirely ignorant.

A large grandfather clock chimed midnight. Gloria pressed the rose and Maureen entered carrying the cake. They all rose except Sophie and sang "Happy Birthday".

Sophie was shocked. She had forgotten that it was her own birthday and yet this funny woman, whom she had met so briefly, had remembered. She fought overwhelming emotion by smoothing her hair, breathing deeply and saying "Wow" and "What a surprise" several times. Adversity was easy to cope with but kindness and an expression of caring friendship was difficult to accept. She was frightened of the childish hopes for continuity or permanence of relationship which was always followed by the pain of being let down. Even the dreaded Rachel was in on the surprise and seemed genuinely happy for her.

"I'm thirty."

"Jesus, what an old lady," Steve laughed.

Gloria was surprised. Sophie's looks and behaviour were more like a teenager than a woman of thirty.

"Don't you dare be so honest, Sophie."

Rachel had reverted back to being the conscientious public relations officer.

"You stay at twenty-nine for at least another five years."

"And then start going backwards, like me."

Gloria was revelling in the successful moment.

"You gotta blow and make a wish Sophie."

"Can we let the candle burn a little bit longer?"

It was the request from a child seeking to extend time.

"Sure we can."

Gloria moved to a seat opposite Sophie and rested her elbows on the table. Together they gazed into the flame. It twisted and soared from the pure white candle, showing a kernel of blue, becoming an aura of red and then merging with the life-giving colour of yellow. A prickling sensation began creeping from just above Gloria's ears towards her temples. Her eyes felt pulled to a third point inside her head, an inner eye that was searching for a link with memory.

The table's polished surface danced with flickering shapes. Faces from the past reached out to her. Steve and Rachel's murmuring voices were joined by other whispered echoes from the past. She looked across the flame to Sophie. A sound slid through her head. It was as if a film negative had been pushed behind her brow and the candle's flame was releasing hidden colour that was building into a picture. Sophie's face registered and then coloured images were pulled violently into her mind. Faces round a camp fire. One particular face, smiling cheekily. The missing piece from the past.

"Meg," she whispered.

It was only Gloria who could faint in a sitting position. Steve knew all the signs and moved quickly to catch her before she hit the floor. He brought her round gently until she opened her eyes, then lifted her back into the chair.

She had no control over her body. Her eyes were staring at Sophie as if seeing her for the first time.

It was Meg. Her face had the same concerned look that she used to see at the summer camps.

"Come on Gloria, I'll look after you. Stick with me. I'll help you Gloria."

"Mouse, come back."

Steve shook her.

"We're having a party, Mouse."

She returned to consciousness and did credit to the early social training in her life by graciously apologising.

"Sorry girls, hope I didn't scare you."

"Yoo hoo, Gloria."

Sophie was too bright and acting her socks off to put her at ease.

"What did you lace the orange juice with?"

"Ah," Gloria bounced back into her stride. "One hundred per cent proof orange."

Rachel decided to take charge and bring the evening back to normality.

"Blow out the candle, Sophie, and make a wish."

The flame was spluttering close to the icing.

Sophie blew and wished that Gloria would always be her friend. One slice of the knife and the fish cake parted to reveal thick cream and sponge.

Gloria merely tasted the cake.

"I'm hyperglycaemic. I've had too much sugar in the pudding already. That's what probably made me faint." She babbled on. "Ninety per cent of alcoholics are hyperglycaemic. Do you know, unless I start the day on protein, I can go into a deep depression. That's why I'm so thin. If I eat too much carbohydrate I start to shake."

"I wish I was a hypergly-whatsit," Sophie moaned. "I have to take these damn Stoller's pills to keep my weight down. I'm so greedy, I love food."

"You're not taking Stoller's pills. Oh God, Sophie, Sarah Woolfe's bowels packed up with those. They're lethal. How long have you been taking them?" Rachel demanded.

"Is that why she pulled out of the T.V. series?"

"She was in hospital six months before they sorted her out."

Sophie had never seen Rachel so agitated.

"Have you got some with you?" Gloria was looking at her intently.

Sophie was frightened. She fumbled in her bag for her pill case.

"These."

She handed them to Gloria who sniffed and then examined them carefully, holding one to the light like a jeweller holding a gem.

"Do you get wheezing in the chest and find it hard to sleep nights?"

"Yes—but I drink some brandy or vodka, that helps."

"Have your nails got all dry?"

"Yes, they keep breaking."

"Jesus Christ, he's giving you amphetamines. No wonder they stop you eating. They're fucking addictive."

"What, like drugs do you mean?" Sophie's eyes were wide with fright.

"They are a goddam drug. Believe me, I'm the expert. I've spent more time in hatches coming off drugs and booze. I know all the thrill pills there are, don't I Steve?"

"Yes dear, I'd say you were a coast to coast connoisseur."

"But they're supposed to be for slimming."

"Sophie, throw them away." Rachel spoke quickly. "I know a model who died from taking them. You remember

Christine Baker, the beautiful girl, on all the covers about two years ago?"

"Was that Stoller's pills?"

"She died of a cerebral haemorrhage. One day that bastard will get charged and sent down, bloody quack."

"I'll get rid of them right now."

Sophie got up from the table and headed towards the hall.

"I'll drop them down the loo," she shouted.

"Thank God you fainted, Gloria," Rachel whispered. "I've often wondered why she was perfectly sweet some days and then a fiend on others. It must have been the pills."

"Well, let's be fair, really. If she were withdrawing on that day, dear, she would be a little paranoid. When I think of the times they've clamped the bars on me and I've withdrawn, I'd say I was just a little schizoid wouldn't you say, Steve?"

"Yes dear, I'd say that. Does she have a drink problem as well Rachel?"

"There have been stories. I've seen her bombed quite a few times."

"That figures." Gloria inhaled deeply and blew a perfect smoke ring.

"Gloria, why don't you warn her about drinking too much?"

"Not tonight. That's a whole new ball game."

Gloria looked at Rachel who was earnestly searching for answers to a problem she would never really understand. But she had a new respect for this large woman who was genuinely trying.

Sophie pushed open the door.

"They keep floating," she giggled nervously, "I had to pull the chain at least three times and each time the water splashed me from the top of the thing."

Exaggerating outrageously, Steve told funny stories about the house's plumbing until they were a noisy, laughing group again. Then followed a conducted tour of the house with Steve describing the history and ghost stories in the best Edgar Wallace tradition.

As they waved goodbye to the shouting visitors, Steve put his arm around Gloria.

"I know why you like Sophie."

"Isn't she great?"

"She's just like you when I first met you; underneath all that noise is just a scared kid."

"It's like watching a part of myself, Steve."

She wanted to tell him about Meg but she didn't know where to begin.

The last embers shuffled in the grate.

"You want a juice, Mouse?"

"Sure."

The fine grey dust packed round the glowing log and formed a pyramid. Gloria stared into the redness trying to recapture the images. She could see Meg smiling, or was it Sophie? The log shifted. Meg rode Trigger and she had Prince who wasn't so frisky. She had been terrified, hanging on to the warm, moving redness as it cantered through the pine forest. Meg had helped her to sit straight so that the other girls didn't laugh at her.

She had fallen off, into some ferns. Meg had picked her up, stopped her being scared and helped her to get back up again.

"What was all this hyperglycaemia bullshit, Mouse?"

Steve handed her a glass and the thoughts winged away.

"It never really bothers you. You only faint like that after eating prawns or when you've got a bug."

He gently scratched her head, releasing the scalp from the tensions of hairpins and lacquer.

"Steve, do you remember there was something I couldn't remember. Even when we first met, I told you there was

58

something from when I was twelve and mother had taken me to that place she said was a holiday home. And it turned out to be a home for wealthy neurotics. Father had spent some time there. Steve, I started to remember the other day but I couldn't remember a name. Someone who meant a lot. Well, tonight, I remembered her name. Meg."

Steve continued to massage her head gently. He had to be cautious. Gloria's childhood was a minefield of incidents, any of which, when dwelt on, could trigger off a relapse. He could hear the tearful note which often preceded a drunken bout.

"Steve, I know that I was being treated for hysterics in that home mother dumped me in. I think they used phenobarbitone or hypnotics to make me forget something. But I could see her tonight, Meg. It's to do with Meg. Sophie is just like her. I want to remember, Steve."

He soothed her with cuddles, while trying to remember everything he had learnt from the Alanon groups he had gone to for advice about how to live with an alcoholic.

"There, there, Mouse, easy does it. We don't have to remember everything at once. A day at a time, Mouse."

He crooned her name and little rhymes she loved. She was his mouse and she needed him. His childhood had been poor but pretty straightforward. The only child of Irish immigrants, he hadn't had many treats but his life had been heaven compared to this poor little rich kid.

After first meeting Gloria at the great coming out party, fate, her family and circumstances had parted them until nineteen fifty-eight when he spotted her in the 21 Club in Manhattan.

Over the years, he had often queried his motives for tying himself up with a kook like Gloria. At the time, he had been attracted by her reputation for being the wild, rich socialite continually in trouble with the cops. But when he had seen her sitting alone and slightly squiffy downstairs in the bar of the 21 Club he knew at once that he needed this outrageous yet vulnerable female to be complete.

She had become the cause in his life, removing the sense of inadequacy he felt as a hack journalist. She was a confused damsel with a dragon for a mother. He had rescued her, only to be caught up in a terrifying sickness. The words "For better or for worse" had haunted him through the years of her overdosing and bout drinking. Sometimes he had been tempted to let an overdose take its natural course but then she would give him that small, tiny mouse look and he would panic at the thought of losing her. When they were together and she was on form, he felt six feet tall. Not five foot five without shoes. A short-arse, as they had called him in the army. She made him feel like the oracle of all knowledge when he helped her with her spelling and typed her letters. They had fought the family and lawyers to get her share of the money. Now he was used to living the life of a man of independent means. He occasionally indulged in some gentle freelance work to keep his hand in and no one shouted, "Move your arse O'Connell." He was no longer just a voyeur reporting other people's lives. He, Steve, was part of a high society story. He would write a book one day about life with Gloria. It would bust the great, snob American social scene wide open. He would write it one day when he found time. It would be a best seller.

"Steve."

"Mmm."

"I will remember, won't I?"

"Sure you will Mouse, easy does it."

"I need you Steve."

"You've got me, Mouse."

*

60

Sophie tried to extend the warmth of the evening. She was even prepared to let the chauffeur go to Jury's Hotel first and drop off Rachel. Anything to delay facing the shabbiness of the cottage.

The air in the lounge was tainted by the smell from empty tuna cans on the kitchen sink. Sophie turned her back on the worn carpet and stained armchairs and fled to the bedroom. Her clothes and shoes were strewn about the floor. Carefully she hung up her coat and began undressing in the dark, taking pleasure in watching the bathroom activities behind neighbours' frosted windows. Bedroom curtains were drawn, depriving her of any shared intimacy. She heard footsteps coming along the lane and stood on the bed for a better view. A young couple paused briefly by the street lamp and then continued on their way. The loneliness began, forcing her back down to the lounge where her night-time partners were waiting. A bottle of vodka and an Edith Piaf record. They transported her to the divine state of shared world pain. She crooned and danced in an applauded ritual to oblivion.

*

Gloria had reached the pleasant drowsy state. Unlike Steve, who dropped off as soon as his head touched the pillow, Gloria liked to listen to his breathing. It always gave her confidence to know that she would not wake up alone. Dreamily she watched the soft clouds scuttling across the dark sky.

"You've got to do it yourself, Gloria."

It was the hottest day of the holiday and Meg wasn't going to help her with the corners of the bed. But she wouldn't get such good marks on her own.

"You'll never learn if I always do it for you."

It was all right for Meg, she was good at everything. Everyone liked her. Her parents kissed and hugged her when they greeted her at Grand Central and this year she had real breasts and wore a bra. Gloria's hadn't developed yet.

Now she was happy. She had Meg all to herself, away from those French girls who only wanted to talk about war. They were looking for flowers for the scrap book.

"Am I still your best friend, Meg?"

"Sure you are, but you've still got to make your own bed."

They found the Creeping Jenny and some violet Twinkle Stars. The tracks were getting steeper as they approached the edge of the forest. There was a stray corn poppy bobbing among the grass. They ran out into the sunshine, each one trying to reach it first.

She could see the grassland curving down towards the cliff. Below, the Hudson River flowed towards the white water and the falls. There was a haze over the distant mountains.

It was there. A brilliant orange swamp lily growing on the steep slope. What was it doing so high up? She tried to reach it.

"I'll get it for you Gloria."

Meg plucked it and held it up. With the other hand she reached to Gloria for help. But Gloria grabbed the lily. There was a tearing sound of roots leaving soil. The splash. The small face floated like a petal along a drain.

"Help me Gloria."

She could hardly breathe. She screamed out, "I'm sorry Meg, I can't . . ."

Steve was shaking her.

"It's all right Mouse. It's only a dream."

"But Steve," Gloria sobbed, "she died for my lily."

Chapter Four

Gloria wandered slowly along the beach marvelling at the smoothness of the shoreline. She felt a great need to understand why her life had been full of traumas and treatment centres. For what purpose? And what was her destiny? In the units, well-meaning Christians had told her about her own crucifixion and possible resurrection. She wondered about the dream. Was that what they meant? To face a horrible truth about herself. That she was a coward. There was no difference between the snivelling twelve-year-old, sucking her thumb in the pine forest, and the forty-two-year-old addict of escapism.

She bent down and picked up a smooth flat stone and threw it, taking careful aim like Steve. It skimmed across the calm sea, leaping three times before sinking. She was a fish, she thought, who had been churned around in life's unfriendly seas, only to be brought to the calm bay of the present. She thought of Sophie's face watching the candle on the cake. She had looked so young and vulnerable. Like a young Meg. She could be as strong as Meg if she weren't caught like a little fish, in a mirror image of Gloria's past.

If she were three years younger, she mused, she could have been my daughter. Her first abortion arranged by Mother had been when she was fifteen. The result of her first drunken party games in the back of a Buick.

She watched the dogs playing with a piece of seaweed.

Ninka scampered back to her and wriggled until Gloria bent down and cuddled her. A tear trickled from behind the dark glasses. She had tried so hard to give Steve a child but there had only been half-formed bloodied lumps. After the sixth attempt, she had been lying in the hospital bed, looking through the window at a stark tree, when she overheard the whispers.

"Well, she's an alcoholic. I guess the kid didn't want to risk it. Fine sort of life it would have had."

She turned back and watched the light trace of her footsteps being washed away by the incoming tide. Another moment in time gone for ever. She knew her history was a succession of broken promises for new beginnings. An urgent need for reparation, an awareness of the passing of time and uncertain future, forced her to take stock of her present situation. How strong was she? If she tried to help Sophie would she, herself, be at risk of drifting back into the madness of addiction? She had only seven, dry, pill-free weeks as an anchor for her own sanity. Would Sophie reject her? But Meg asked for help through Sophie's eyes. The thought of Meg made her cry. A part of herself was forever floating too far from reach. She found a dry rock and sat down, letting the tears cloud her glasses. The dogs scampered over, worried by the soft, mewling sounds. Sympathetic cries echoed from gulls following a distant fishing boat.

Gloria took off her glasses and allowed the fresh air to cool her eyes. Through her blurred vision she could make out the shapes of two fishermen in a dinghy pulling in a net. She replaced the glasses and watched the men working slowly and methodically shouting encouragement to each other. She needed to help Sophie. She felt a kind of detached love for her and a desperate desire to express it. It was unlike anything she had felt before.

The cynical part of Gloria said, "Holy Mother Ireland

has got ya" but the long lost Gloria of Camp Happy days listened to the call from Meg: "Come on Gloria, you can do it."

"Sophie could be strong like you, Meg." She talked to the air. The dogs pulled at her cardigan. Her knees and neck ached and the house seemed far away.

"If I can make it back to the house, I can help her." She clambered across the pebbles, Meg's voice winding in and out of her memory.

"If you get to this bush, it's only a short step to this easy path. All right Gloria, I'll help you."

Each step of the way helped to create a zealot. She reached the house and collected will-power as a prize.

Steve greeted her with concern.

"Are you okay Mouse?"

"Let go, Steve. I'm fine."

*

Sophie woke at two o'clock in the afternoon with an insatiable oral yearning. A pint of water couldn't quench her thirst. Her whole body felt dehydrated. She ran up to the delicatessen and staggered back with juices, vodka and a selection of food. After stuffing three yoghurts, some soda bread, butter and jam, she knocked back vodka and orange juice and sat bloated, in a state of bliss. Pleasant thoughts of tidying the cottage and then heading for the pub to listen to the Kerry Slides gave way to morbidity when Maggie called.

The vibrations from her mother's voice reached down the telephone to grab Sophie by the throat. She nagged about her arthritis and about how hard it was to manage now that Percy had left her. This was followed by a violent diatribe about Percy's new girlfriend and a request for money. Her salacious curiosity about Sophie's sex life brought a defiant response.

"I'm fucking like a rabbit. That's all I do—haven't time for work."

Then the row. The reminder that there was her mother living without the necessities of life while her famous daughter cavorted around the world. What would the papers say if they knew? The symbol of motherhood hit a bullseye and Sophie renounced femininity, her mother's image forever in her brain.

Hardly had she finished with Maggie and picked up another glass of vodka when Aunt Nell phoned.

"Sophie, thought you ought to know luv, yer Dad's coming out in June . . ."

"I know."

"Well, Soph, he's going to need a bit of help to get going."

Sophie waited.

"Are you there Sophie?"

"Yes."

"Well as I was saying, he'll have nowhere to live. There's no room here with Jack and the kids. If you're not using your flat . . ."

"I will be."

"Oh." There was a long sigh. "He thinks a lot of you Sophie."

"Oh yes?"

"He's very proud of you Sophie. Never talks about you inside though."

She whispered the word inside as though the Special Branch were listening.

"I'll fix him up, don't worry Nell."

She couldn't go to Dartmoor to collect him. She had visited once in nineteen fifty-nine. The memory of the grim, forbidding place with its atmosphere of hopeless depression had given her nightmares for weeks.

"All right, are you?"

"Fine."

"I'll be going then."

"Bye."

She ran out into the front courtyard in a feverish attempt to shake off the suffocating family tentacles.

"It's Sophie isn't it?"

His grey beard was caught up in a clothes peg. Blue eyes smiled from a small dignified face. He was balanced on a ladder, scooping out leaves from the guttering. Sophie thought he looked about seventy.

"You're a Russian priest or something, aren't you?"

He adjusted the clothes peg.

"In exile, yes."

"Well, perhaps you as a priest can tell me why we have to honour our fathers and mothers."

She tried to sound jovial.

"Are you having trouble with your parents?"

"You're joking; just all my life, that's all."

The priest could hear the bitterness in her voice.

"What do I call you, father, brother or what?"

"Why don't you call me Vladimir. That's my name."

Sophie moved closer to the wall. He peered down at her and laughed.

"How old are you?"

"Thirty yesterday."

"Ah, the feast day of Bishop Mesrop, a servant of knowledge."

He studied her face. She had a slightly Slav look about her and looked uncannily like his friend Alexis who had died in Solovetzk.

"And you are thirty. The time we ask big questions and search for a philosophy to understand why we ask them." He chuckled.

Sophie knew he was about to say something profound and

became uneasy. She watched him clearing more wet leaves. He exuded an air of peace and serenity. She smiled ruefully, knowing that she wasn't ready to listen or give up her anger.

"I must go in now."

"Come and visit me sometime."

"I'll do that."

The priest caught the whimsical smile before she slouched off. It was another glimpse of Alexis. The young priest murdered in nineteen twenty-five. He had been shot when he swam into the White Sea, trying to escape his torturers. He, Vladimir, had been on his way through Europe when he heard. He had often wondered why Tikhon, the wonderful old Patriarch of all Russia, had instructed him to leave for Europe while the sweet, gentle Alexis had remained behind.

*

Late Friday afternoon, Michael drove Gloria to Sophie's cottage. It was not far from the American Embassy.

Gloria found Sophie leaping around in a kimono. *Hair* music boomed out into the mews, shattering the quiet of the soft, Irish dusk. From the cottage next door came the sound of a man's voice chanting on a single note. Gloria felt as if she had been transported back to Greenwich Village. She instructed Michael to return in an hour. She wasn't quite sure whether she could cope for longer. Sophie was obviously as high as a skunk.

She perched on an armchair while Sophie fetched her some orange juice.

"To a friendly fish."

"Cheers."

Sophie paced the room.

"You're my friend. Can you understand when I say that I hate my mother?" She stood, challenging Gloria for a reaction. "Does that shock you?"

The American looked up in surprise. "Hell no. I hate mine too. She's a bitch of a slut."

Sophie sighed.

"Oh listen Sophie dear, there is nothing you can teach me about hating your mother. Mine just destroys me. One look from her and I turn to stone."

Sophie curled up at Gloria's feet, grateful for the chance to share her woes. "You know, she has never ever cuddled me. Every time I tried, she pushed me away. Nothing I have ever done or achieved has pleased her."

Sophie continued to pour out the hurt. Gloria felt close to tears. Apart from the differences in environment, it was like hearing her own childhood experiences. Sophie's sense of timing twisted the misery into wry humour.

"No wonder she resents me. I was a Volpar Gel pessary that didn't work, so she told me. I am the great, living jelly baby that got in the way and forced her to marry my Dad."

"Sophie."

Sophie stopped ranting and listened.

"When I was twenty-one, I inherited a million bucks from my grandmother, that is on my father's side."

"A million, wow."

"Do you know what my mother did? She got these guys to follow me and catch me on a drunk. And then they all got me to sign away the money to her. How's that for mother love?"

Sophie groaned.

"She hated me. The only reason I was born was so she could keep a hold on my father. She married him for his money, of course. Gossip says she's great in the feathers but she certainly never made out as a lady. That's why she hated me, because I was brought up in the old family tradition. The right schools and so on. That bitch had me put away in so many institutions."

"But what about your father, couldn't he . . ."

69

"Dear, he spent a lot of time in these ritzy 'laughing farms'. He is an alcoholic, like most of his family. They say kids of alcoholics either become one or marry one."

"But . . ."

"It was Steve who finally got me out and away from her."

Gloria went into more lurid details of her family feud. Sophie listened with compassion and reached out to comfort the little woman.

"Did she turn you into an alcoholic, Gloria?"

Gloria paused and rummaged in her bag for a tissue, while her brain ticked over.

"No dear."

She blew her nose hard, remembering the purpose of the visit, then casually lit a Gauloise.

"I mean she sure as hell gave me some personality problems but it was alcohol that made an alcoholic—you know some of us are just allergic to the stuff."

"What do you mean allergic?"

Gloria felt she was treading on egg shells. She chose her words carefully. "Well dear, some of us are born with a central nervous system that can't cope with it—I think we're usually more sensitive than the average guys."

"How do you mean more sensitive?"

"Well." She racked her brain for all the analogies used by the counsellors. "Let's say, we always feel things more intensely. I mean look at . . ." She searched for classy examples. "Scott Fitzgerald, I mean, how many more books would that guy have written if he'd kicked it. Look at Monroe, Buster Keaton . . ."

Gloria watched Sophie's expression change from one of curiosity to one of interest. She decided not to overdo it.

"Could you tell if someone was alcoholic, Gloria?" Sophie was being over-casual. Gloria felt a streak of wickedness.

"Oh yes."

"How?"

"By the very way they hold their glass."

Sophie spilt the vodka with fright.

Gloria continued ruthlessly. "You should see some of the gals in the hatches. Red veins all over their faces, puffy, bloodshot eyes. And then, of course, there's the brain damage."

"Shit, what's that?"

"Well dear, every blackout destroys a brain cell and they don't replace themselves, you know."

"Christ." Sophie put down her glass. "What's a blackout?"

"It's when you can't remember what you did when you were drunk."

"Oh."

Sophie was silent. Gloria had hit home. The doorbell broke the silence. It was Michael come to take her home.

Gloria felt tranquil but not tired. Steve noticed her new confidence as she described her strategy with Sophie. He was curious about the similarity between the two women and amazed at Gloria's sense of objectivity. They talked until nearly dawn when Steve retired. She waited, watching the surge of wind brushing the trees and listening to the birds announcing the daybreak. Her promise would be fulfilled. She may not have stopped Sophie yet, but she sure as hell had ruined her drinking. She'd thrown out the bait and if Sophie was half the girl she thought she was, she'd bite.

The call came on Sunday afternoon.

"Hello Gloria."

"Sophie."

"Ah . . . I was wondering . . . ah, I think I might be a bit of an alcoholic."

"Really?"

"Do you think I am?"

"Oh, no dear. I'm sure you're not. I mean, you don't have blackouts or drink a lot, do you?"

"Ah. Sometimes, a bit."

"Oh, I'm sure you're not. I mean anyone who can do the three drink test isn't."

"What's that?"

"Well dear, if anyone can just drink three drinks a day, no more and no less, then they definitely don't have a problem."

"Three?"

"Three."

"How big a glass?"

"Regular size."

"Ah. It was nice seeing you the other night."

"Yeh. Let's get together again soon."

"Yes."

Sophie put down the phone and returned to the mirror to stare again at the tiny, red vein just by her nose. She examined her eyes but they weren't bloodshot, just yellow. She had slept until three when the sound of Vladimir's singing woke her to confusion.

She looked through the kitchen cupboard and found three large tumblers. Gloria had said three. No more, no less. She lined them up along the draining board. She reasoned that as Gloria had referred to alcohol, orange juice could be added. Then the drinks would last longer. She spent half an hour first measuring the vodka into the tumblers, then transferring it into a jug before mixing in the orange juice.

The first gulp brought her body back to life. There was still a little daylight so she decided to walk. Seven hours to go before her compulsory bedtime. The car was picking her up for work at six thirty in the morning.

She walked up Raglan Lane towards Clyde Road, then turned right in the direction of Pembroke Park. She was unaware of the exquisite iron railings, the neat gardens with clumps of snowdrops and the occasional crocus; her brain was preoccupied with the division of time into liquid measurement. The street lights came on suddenly and she found she had walked in a complete circle. A westerly wind had chilled her face and ears. Her stomach squeezed reminding her that she had not eaten. Numb legs carried her along the uneven lane towards the cottage. As she grew nearer she could see the lights in Vladimir's window and could smell the aroma of cooking. Cautiously, like a stray cat, she approached his front door.

She watched his reaction carefully but he seemed genuinely pleased to see her. Gratefully she accepted his invitation to join him for supper. Without the aid of Stoller's pills to suppress her appetite, she was almost dribbling in anticipation. Oblivious to any detail in the room, her eyes searched for the source of the delicious smell. There was a casserole of fish and potato stew on the table and a loaf of black bread.

The priest drew up a chair for her, then went to the sideboard for another plate. He noticed that she was shivering so threw some more peat on the fire. He saw the dark shadows under her eyes and wondered what troubled her.

Her hunger satisfied, Sophie turned her attention to her surroundings. The softly lit room was lined with books and tapestries. In one corner stood an ornate, brass ornament. It had a column wrought in intricate filigree supporting a triangle, inside which was a black circle with two crescent moons surrounded by fine gold tapestry. Behind this, in an alcove, lit by a red glass lamp, was a small icon of a black madonna. The warm red rays from the corner enhanced the peaceful atmosphere of the room. The nagging urge for a drink interfered with her concentration on Vladimir's softly spoken conversation.

"To leave the country of one's mother-tongue when there

73

is a need to express thoughts and philosophy is indeed an exile—but then I have learnt the value of silence which I might otherwise not have learnt . . ."

He began to show her pictures of the monastery of the Holy Trinity and Saint Sergius in Zagorsk, the place of his young priesthood.

Sophie began to twitch. He sensed her lack of attention and apologised for talking too much. Sophie felt ashamed and attempted to explain about her experiment with the three drinks. The priest looked at her closely and understood her dilemma. He had seen the empty bottles lined up in her backyard and had suspected that she shared the problem so common in Ireland.

"Sophie, this friend of yours—she can help you with the fight with the vodka?"

She became nervous and tried joking about the fact that she and Gloria were two fish.

His eyes softened. "Yes, indeed you are."

He clasped his hands and stared into the fire.

"You understand Sophie, that when people fight this kind of problem—it is also a sickness of the innermost self."

He looked back to her to see if she was listening. The high, Slav cheekbones were emphasised by the light from the fire. She had the same blue eyes as Alexis. He looked at her intently.

"You see Sophie, the inner self can only reach your mind and speak to you if your mind is clear and able to listen —vodka can deny you this rapport with your true self."

Sophie was pulled two ways. Part of her cried to stay with this warm, tender man and listen to the promise of alternative living but the other nature fought to cling to the way of indifference. The vodka won. She excused herself, thanking him profusely for the supper. She lowered her eyes as she assured him that her early call the following morning was the reason for her departure.

"Come and see me anytime, Sophie."

"Cheers, Vladimir."

It had to last five hours.

"Je ne regrette rien," wailed through the cottage as she eked out the remaining vodka.

She woke in the early hours with cramp in the stomach and wondered whether it was a heart attack. Her nightdress was soaked and her throat parched. She strained her eyes to see the time. The numbers on the alarm clock blurred and moved about. She squeezed her lids tight. Lights were flashing in her head. Three o'clock. She panicked. Only three hours before she had to get up. She felt exhausted, yet too frightened to sleep. She stumbled out of bed and held on to the cold door. Her chest began to tighten.

She found the brandy and took a couple of slugs. The panic went. The liquid warmed her chest and eased her throat muscles. She continued to sip from the bottle until the thought struck her that she had failed the three drink test. She rationalised that a bad night didn't count. She could try again tomorrow. She staggered back to bed and slept with the light on.

*

Gloria waited. She and Steve had discussed the need for Sophie to be dried out but agreed that a clinic would attract too much attention. It was decided that if she asked for help they would look after her at De Courcy House.

"It's better for her to go cold turkey if she can stand it Steve."

"I don't know. What if she goes into the DTs?"

"She's not chronic, Steve. Not far off, but, no, it'll be rough

75

but she'll survive. We don't want them sticking her on pills."

The days passed.

On the third of March, they celebrated Steve's birthday quietly at the Russell Hotel.

On Friday, the thirteenth of March, the flowers arrived. The call came later.

"Happy Birthday, Gloria."

"Sophie. Thank you for the lovely flowers. Where are you?"

"I'm in the harbour pub in Balbriggan, we're shooting in Seapoint Lane."

Gloria could hear the sound of defeat in her voice.

"It's my last day on this set-up, then all my scenes are by Dublin docks."

"Are you okay Sophie?"

Gloria heard a sniffle then a fumbling as Sophie covered the mouthpiece. There was a long pause.

"I can't do the test, Gloria. I don't know which drink does it . . ."

"The first."

"Pardon?"

"What are you doing after work Sophie?"

"Nothing."

There was a sob.

"Why don't you come and stay for the weekend?"

"Can I?"

"I've got everything you need. Just come straight over."

"Thank you Gloria."

Steve watched Gloria galvanising Mary into action. He had expected a mournful discussion about the need for a face lift or a non stop interrogation about how attractive she still was and how young she looked. That was the usual birthday routine. And now, here was his Gloria totally oblivious of herself, concentrating on another person's problems. He felt almost jealous. He couldn't ever remember her putting herself out for him like this.

"Steve, do you think we ought to warn Dr Hennessy that we have a friend staying who might need attention? What do you think?"

"Sure, assuming she comes off the booze dear. She may not fit in with your plans for her."

"She will."

Steve was taken back. For a moment Gloria had sounded just like old man Van Heerden, when he was on form.

Sophie arrived at six looking wan. She was hesitant as she greeted Steve. He watched like an outsider as Gloria ushered her into the house. The women were sharing an understanding of which he was no part. Throughout the evening he served them coffee and tea. The only break in their earnest discussion was for supper when he joined them briefly for a gossip about the studio. Gloria had become detached from him, he thought, watching them return to the lounge. He felt terribly alone. He thought of the large bottle of Jungle Gardenia which he had arranged to be sent over from Sachs of Fifth Avenue for her birthday. It was the smell that brought back memories of their first meeting in the 21 Club. He had wanted her to wear it tonight so that he could be really roused.

He took some fruit juices to them. Sophie was chain smoking, getting in and out of the chair and twiddling with the buttons on her shirt. All the signs he'd seen before with Gloria.

"Steve, Sophie's going to try getting through twenty-four hours without a drink. She can do it, can't she?"

77

"Sure you can Sophie. If Gloria can do it, anyone can."

He smiled at Sophie. Large, fearful eyes looked back. He had seen that same expression on Gloria's face over the years.

"Well girls, I'm turning in now."

"Goodnight Steve. Thank you for letting me stay."

He wandered up the stairs. It was going to be a long disturbed night. Perhaps he would try reading.

Gloria behaved like a mother with a newly born baby. Every cough or sound from Sophie's room and she was out of bed like a jackrabbit.

Sophie was experiencing a strange dream. Gloria hovered as the girl muttered and twisted in her sleep. Sophie found herself running through woods. She was trying to reach a cave. A man with a white face was following behind. He had no hair and she was frightened of seeing his eyes. In the distance, in the side of a mountain, she could see the cave. Inside there were flickering candles and she knew that the answer to life was there. She began climbing when the ground gave way and she was falling. She found herself in fast-moving water. The white face swam towards her.

"Help me, I'm drowning."

Gloria was shocked rigid. "It's all right Meg, I'm here. I'm here." She calmed down and shook herself free from the past, busying herself by holding a damp cloth over Sophie's brow.

"It's all right Sophie, it's a dream."

Sophie's eyes were glazed. She could vaguely hear Gloria. She seemed to be behind a sheet of water. She turned back to look at the woods. There was someone just behind the trees. A soft voice whispered, "Breathing is the natural way to the heart."

She began deep breathing and then she was through the sheet of water and looking at Gloria's worried face.

"I'm thirsty."

"Here."

"What is it?"

"Water."

Gloria helped her to sip from a red glass tumbler. The light from the bedside lamp shone through it. Sophie smiled with some inner secret and fell into a peaceful sleep.

Gloria switched off the light. A part of the battle was over. The two of them against John Barleycorn. She shut the door quietly and made her way downstairs.

Steve didn't hear her approach. He was by the fire, a book on his knees, crying. The sight shocked her.

"Steve."

He turned away. Gloria was mortified at the sight of his trembling lower lip.

"Steve. What's up?"

" 'S nothing."

"Steve," she wailed. "What's wrong?"

"It's just . . ." He tried to regain his composure and failed.

"Oh Mouse, I was reliving your times . . . I always felt so lonely . . . Each time you kind of went away . . . A stranger was in your body."

Gloria felt a deep shame. She had relied on Steve for all these years and hardly considered his feelings. She had trampled over his emotions while squealing about her own sensitivity. Her life's preoccupation was unravelling itself to expose her complete self-centredness.

She held him tightly to her breast and tried to squeeze her gratitude into his shoulders.

"I'm all right now."

He struggled for the old relationship. She hung on.

"I love you Steve. I wish I could undo the past. I've never wanted to hurt you. I'm sorry."

"Oh Mouse."

He looked at her angrily.

"Of course it hurts. How do you think I feel when you go on another bender? I blame myself. I wonder where I've failed you. I wonder if it's something about us that you're trying to escape." She crawled on to his knee and handed him back his role as master.

The woods were silent. All Sophie could hear was her own steady breathing. She found the cave, lifted her arms and flew to the entrance. She passed through rows of flaming candles to dark space and holy stillness. At the end of the darkness was a solitary flame in red glass. As she drew nearer she saw the sweet smile of the Madonna.

Saturday was an eternity of denial. Time had to be filled with every form of activity and a demanding gullet had to be filled with various beverages. Steve marched her along the beach when it sounded as if someone was breaking every bone in her head. Her fingertips hurt and her brain and mouth were unconnected. The night came and it was as if a wad of cotton wool had fallen out of her ears. She could hear everything in the world moving. She took three baths to fill in time and rediscovered her skin's reaction to temperature.

On Sunday, she woke to the sound of church bells and depression. Sunday was the end of the week. Rain drummed against the windows and thirty was a long time of living. Reality was seeing the dust on the window sill.

Her appetite was enormous. She devoured lunch and was amused at the thought of changing shape during the dock scenes. Gloria and Steve were relieved at her change of mood.

When it was time to leave, she clung to them both.

"If you get the yang yangs, call me, Sophie."

"I will."

She started towards the car.

"Thank you, both of you."

She had hardly entered the cottage when Vladimir was knocking on the door.

"Are you all right, Sophie?"

She apologised for the untidy room.

"I've been away for the weekend with my friends. I've dried out, Vladimir. Come off the vodka."

"Spasiba za atvyet na malyeniya," he whispered. "What time do they come for you tomorrow Sophie?"

"Six."

"Now, I have a suggestion. Please, I hope you will not take offence."

"What?"

"Leave your keys with me when you go and permit me to tidy up the house for you."

"Oh no . . ."

"Listen Sophie. You have undertaken a courageous thing —to fight the vodka. Permit me, as your friend, to help make life a little easier for you. If our Lord could wash feet, is Vladimir too proud to wash a floor, no?"

"My feet are clean," Sophie giggled. "I've had so many baths to fill in the time."

He was glad she was able to laugh. He talked with her until he was satisfied that she was safe to be left alone.

"Think of one thing Sophie, when you are working tomorrow."

"Mmm."

"The world was given light. That light shows itself through colour. Look for the colour, Sophie, and really see."

"I'll try."

She lay in bed waiting for sleep. Her mind was a jumble of thoughts. She wondered what she had ever done in her life to deserve three such good friends.

She woke before the alarm. The driver was shocked to find her waiting for him. It was usual for him to hammer on the door to hurry her or on bad days, drive to the nearest phone box and call her. She sat hunched up in the back of the car trying to remember her lines and finding it difficult to concentrate.

The docks had been transformed into the nineteen twenties. Men were still putting the finishing touches to the brickwork. Under huge colonnades of rusting iron lay the cobbled wharfside. Shire horses were being pulled along slabbed tracks from a past era. Sophie was dropped at her caravan from where she could see the director striding about in an Arran sweater and speaking phony Irish. Local extras, grouped around the catering van, watched silently as their language was bastardised. Ich bin ein Berliner, Sophie thought sourly.

"Your eyes are looking a lot better Sophie. Have you been a good girl and had an early night?"

Sophie looked in the mirror. Bill was right. The puffiness had gone. The make-up man was relieved; for once he wouldn't have to put on an ice pack.

She was glad that he was speaking quietly. It was as if the whole world had turned up the sound. She rested her head back in the chair trying not to listen to all the activity outside. The individual shouts, the rumblings of equipment and distant early morning traffic. With all that and the continual touching of her face, she couldn't hold on to the lines.

In the scene she had to distract the soldiers while guns were being shifted from the barge. Every footstep on the cobbles jarred her jaw. Seagulls screamed as they hovered over the breakfast remains. Pigeons crooned in small turrets, jutting out over the water. They rehearsed over and over again.

She remembered Vladimir's words and tried to focus on colour and detail. Each item became her anchor of sanity —the sacks laid carefully along the wharf, a cane basket, and an old oil drum with ALL FAGENDS AND RUBBISH IN HERE, made it possible to remember the lines. Moira stood in for her when they were ready to light and Sophie managed to escape to a quiet corner.

She found a backwater, away from the frantic activity. An occasional member of the crew hurried past to fetch some equipment and looked at her curiously. It was not usual for Sophie Smith to come out of her caravan. She was oblivious to the glances. Her attention was on the water and the world reflected in it. She saw the colours and shapes of the mirrored buildings and again remembered the old priest's words: "Look for the colour Sophie and really see."

By lunchtime she had completed the master shot and all her close-ups. She had a break before her next scene. The next set-up was with the animals. Already the trainers were rehearsing with the dogs and shires.

"You're very quiet today Sophie. Anything worrying you?"

The director approached her with tact.

"I'm fine. Did that scene work for you?"

"Great. I loved that reaction you gave Tim. Really worked well."

"Good. How long have I got because I've got a change?"

"A good couple of hours. The lady with the dogs doesn't seem to have them very much under control. And you're fine?"

"Really."

It was better inside the caravan. The noise was slightly muffled. She looked down at her hands. They were shaking.

A tray had been left for her. She ate all the food but sniffed cautiously at the flask of coffee, in case Moira had been generous and added Irish whiskey. Certain of her safety, she gulped down the hot liquid. Her throat insatiably demanded the swallowing sensation.

Some workers from nearby gathered on the opposite wharf to watch the unusual activity. Sophie watched them sitting in the lukewarm sunshine, their arms resting on their knees. Some ate sandwiches, others just stared waiting for something to happen. Eventually they became bored with the repetition and issued a series of cat calls, farmyard noises and insults. The sparks and other men on the unit retaliated gleefully with threatening signals and noises. Sophie was fascinated by the two groups of men and their primitive behaviour.

The unease began at three o'clock in Gladys' and Clara's caravan, while her hair was being checked. The smell of whiskey on Clara's breath began to disturb her. She caught sight of the bottles by the Carmen curlers and began to get tetchy with the chattering woman. Her head was sensitive to the incessant fumblings. It was hard to keep her feet still and she felt a great urge to scream. Divine intervention came when Gloria popped her head round the door.

"Hi Sophie."

She hugged the American. Never had she been so glad to see anyone. The hairdressers exchanged looks of surprise. Sophie Smith wasn't known to be so demonstrative. They stared inquisitively at the thin, strange blonde woman.

"We were shopping in town and I spotted this and thought, I guess Sophie could do with some Joy in her life right now."

Gloria winked as she handed over a large box of Joy cologne. The two women roared with laughter. Gloria's loud voice started off a yelping from the dogs on the set. There were shouts of "*Quiet over there*" from the first assistant and the two culprits fled to Sophie's caravan. Steve was with Rachel by the cameras. He slunk into his collar, disowning the blonde noisy broad with the voice like a jackass.

"You've got to get organised for when the big thirst starts."

Gloria produced a selection of tonics, orange and bitter lemons.

Sophie felt a delicious madness. The irritability had been replaced by a sense of zany sisterhood and a feeling of belonging that she had sought from drink and never found.

Gloria watched with pride as Sophie performed in front of the camera. The girl could lick the problem. Steve squeezed her hand.

"You've done a good job there, Mouse."

At last she knew the happiness of achievement. If she died tomorrow, she thought, she had done something good in her life.

Vladimir was there to welcome Sophie home. The old priest ushered her into a transformed cottage. A vase of daffodils stood in the centre of the table on which he had laid out some fruit, cheese and bread. Sophie bowed her head, overcome with all the kind friendship she'd received during the day. The old man moved about silently, understanding her need for quiet. He stayed for an hour, listening attentively to her discoveries and experiences. When he laughed with her, she felt a freedom and when eventually he left, she realised, for one second in time, the meaning of peace.

Each following day became a lesson in the art of living. Gloria kept cheering her on and added humour to a sometimes painful reality. In the evenings, Sophie was able to share the more sensitive side of herself with Vladimir.

When at last she said: "Vladimir, right at this moment I am happy. That has never happened to me before. It's always been—I remember being happy or I shall be happy when . . . But I have never known what it is to be happy in the moment."

The old priest looked and saw that the haunted look in her

85

eyes had been replaced by the trusting look of a child. She was allowing herself to be vulnerable.

"Our destiny shows itself all through our life," he said. "But the joy is, when we have the courage to go and meet it."

The last day of filming came too quickly and she was overwhelmed by the fact that people were sorry to see her leave. She was given unexpected presents and cried because she knew she was liked for herself and not for her fame.

She was to fly back to London to start work immediately at Shepperton Studios. For three months she would be playing opposite a famous American comedy actor. Jacob was over the moon, having increased her salary and won her billing over the title, the same size as the famous American.

Gloria and Steve accompanied her to the airport.

"Goodbye Fish, I shall miss you."

"Steve and I will be over soon, won't we Steve?"

"Yes dear."

"We're going to book into the Ritz for a couple of days. We'll let you know when."

Gloria cuddled her. "I'm so proud of you Sophie."

Sophie put on her dark glasses. Her bottom lip was trembling. "Bye," she whispered and fled into the airport.

Gloria blew her nose.

"Don't worry Mouse, we'll see her soon."

PART TWO

Chapter Five

Sophie's kitchen window overlooked the forecourt of Nell Gwynn House. She stood watching the birds swooping past cars and returning to the trees that lined Sloane Avenue. Their wheeling and incessant noise reminded her that it was spring and that she was too tired to take part.

Since returning from Dublin a schedule of dress fittings, make-up tests and newspaper interviews had exhausted her. Apart from a dinner with Jacob and Henry there had been no time to relax. She was sick of the studio chat and missed the peaceful discussions with Vladimir.

A sleek studio car pulled up in front of the building. Jacob was inside ready to escort her to the pre-film "get-together". He was always five minutes early. She could see the top of his grey head as he entered the foyer. She checked her make-up before going down to meet him.

"You look a picture." He kissed her cheek. "The Caprice please, driver."

The chauffeur did not have to be told. He had his instructions from the studio. Sophie watched Jacob fuss over her dress and relieve her of her handbag and jacket. He seemed to have aged. Even his movements had become slower. He had always been a dapper little man with quick speech and expressive hands. It alarmed her to think of him as old.

Jacob had worried ever since Sophie had told him about the effects of Stoller's pills and drink on her. He and Henry had consulted a friend who was a specialist at Warlingham Park Hospital. He had suggested that she take a course of vitamin B12 and a holiday. She did look tired. Jacob was torn between being a good agent and a loving friend. He would like to have said, "Sophie get out now. Find yourself a nice man, have children and lead a happy, uncomplicated life." But he also knew that her career was at a point where she could reach for international stardom. She was thirty but looked younger. One mistake now and she would be stuck with supporting roles. Inwardly he fretted. He didn't want to push her too hard.

The drinks party was from six until seven-thirty. There was dinner afterwards for the chosen few. The drill at these gatherings was that Jacob would stay with Sophie until he was satisfied that she was relaxed with someone then he would embark on a round of hustling.

Everyone in the room was intent on making a good first impression. Models playing small parts stood eating crisps carefully and licking their lips between bites. Actors with gleaming white teeth which could never survive the ordeal of eating an apple said "Pleased to meet you" and looked over her shoulder. Some had carefully unbuttoned shirts, displaying their masculinity to those who might be interested. The publicity man smoked a large cigar and looked like Groucho Marx. The director fawned over older stars, reassuring them of their illustrious pasts. Hank Schwartz, her co-star, was relaxed and friendly.

"I knew when Freddy showed me your rushes we'd get on just great. Don't you think it's a great script?"

"Great." Sophie tried to look enthusiastic. She had christened the film "The Anniversary Schmaltz". The script was undiluted drivel. A storyline preoccupied with a middle-aged man's attempts at extra marital sex. After all the tits and titillation, he realises that marriage is the most important

thing in his life. Cue for soft focus and violins. Jacob assured
her that it would be a box office success and urged her to
accept it. She knew he was right. The name Hank Schwartz
drew large cinema audiences all over the world. She was to
play Norma, the naive, dizzy wife. All her scenes involved
plot so she couldn't be edited out.

"Sophie, you'll have to help me out tomorrow." Hank led
her away from the collective small talk. "Er, this bed scene.
Hell, they would start the film with that. I've never done a bed
scene before."

"It's not a love scene, Hank, we're just eating breakfast."

"Yeah, but you know what I mean."

"Don't worry, just think of me as a plate of meat."

"I can't do that Sophie."

"Why not?"

"Because I'm a vegetarian."

A flashlight recorded their moment of laughter.

The round table was laid for twelve. Hank sat next to her.
She felt at ease with the warm-hearted, chubby little man. She
noticed that he didn't drink heavily like most of the others.
The champagne began to pop. A toast to the production. She
heard herself refusing and became embarrassed.

The man opposite her ordered some Perrier. "Would you
care for some, Sophie?" he asked.

She looked into brown, slightly Asiatic eyes.

"That would be just fine."

During the meal he kept glancing towards her. Not flirting,
just offering an alternative to the personality promotion
around the table. Coffee arrived and seats were swopped to
emphasise ideas and arguments. He was about five-feet-ten
with soft, collar-length brown hair. He moved gracefully, like
a cat, into the seat beside her.

"The way you're slugging down the Perrier and chewing
those cigarettes makes me think you could be an ex-drunk

like me, am I right?" Sophie looked round in case anyone had heard. He looked amused.

"Yes."

He watched her light another cigarette. "How long have you been off it?"

"About three weeks."

"You're doing very well."

"Thank you kind sir, she said."

He smiled. "I shall be watching your performance very carefully."

"Oh yes."

"I add the music."

"You're a composer."

"God, you're quick."

She laughed.

He talked easily about his work and life. His warm resonant voice had a soothing effect but it was his gentleness that overwhelmed her. When he smiled his face revealed a sweetness unusual in a man. She had a strong desire to touch the defined line around his mouth.

His name was Mike Bonnaire. The Asiatic look came from a grandfather who had arrived in Liverpool from somewhere in Europe and in family photographs looked like a gypsy.

He had been divorced for some time but a year ago had ended an affair with a singer. His expression changed as he spoke about the passionate relationship that had involved drugs.

They had both become wrecks and had been sent to a unit. He had managed to kick the drugs but turned to alcohol, recovering from that with the help of group therapy. She had been unable to come off drugs so they had parted. Sophie felt the pain in his voice and took his hand. His palm was dry and smooth and she was reluctant to let go when their space was invaded by the speeded-up tempo of show business conversation.

As she left he called across to her.

"See you at the studios, Sophie."

"See you."

As the car drove her along wet Chelsea streets, she felt like a highly tuned violin pitched for the highest note. Outside Nell Gwynn House she breathed in deeply the freshly washed air and looked up to the trees where pigeons were crooning and scuffling. She too felt part of spring.

Hank's delivery was fast and his comedy business inspired. Sophie found his rhythm and threw him his lines, feeding him brilliantly. When the final take ended the crew applauded them both. Hank was as thrilled as a child.

"I guess they really liked that scene Sophie. The dresser guy said they don't do that too often. Is that right?"

"Not often. It's got to be really good to get them going."

"Is that so?"

Sophie continued to reassure him all the way back to the dressing rooms. As they parted company she noticed the sweat above his lip and his hand shaking as he unlocked his door. The casual Hank Schwartz was a full-time act, she thought. The real Hank was terrified and well hidden by a large smile.

Later, she knocked at his door to see whether he wanted to join her for lunch. The sweet smell hit her when she entered the room.

"Want a joint kid?"

"No thanks Hank, I'm going to the restaurant. Are you eating?"

"They're fetching me an omelette. Catch up with you later."

He was smiling and relaxed again.

It was part of Sophie's contract that a table was permanently reserved for her to be cancelled only on her instructions. It was one of the many indications of star status in the studios. She fingered the shiny cutlery resting on the white starched tablecloth and watched the activity on the other tables. Publicity directors lunching with feature writers, casting directors, casts from other productions, people acknowledging each other. She returned a few smiles then hid behind the menu. Her appetite had left her and she felt let down by Hank.

"Do you want to be alone and thoughtful or would you like my company?"

"Oh yes."

"Yes what?"

"I need your company."

The warm dry palm was instant security. In the daylight, his skin had the slightly sallow hue of a Eurasian and his eyes seemed lighter amber, like the colour of a tiger.

"What's wrong?"

"Oh Mike, Hank's on pot."

"Yes I know but I think he can handle it. On the whole this company is relatively together. The other two productions have got real problems. That lot there are pissed from lunch onwards and the other bunch have three of the leads mainlining."

"Jesus, it's like a creeping fungus."

He squeezed her hand reassuringly.

"Don't let it worry you. I hear your scene went really well this morning."

"Yes."

Her hand was released so she fiddled with the cutlery.

"Does it bother you Mike, all this drugs and booze?"

He watched her drawing patterns on the tablecloth with the knife.

"I'll tell you what I'm going to do for you. Do you have a tape recorder?"

"No."

"I'll get you one. I'm going to make you a set of tapes and when anything gets to you—you play a tape and it will take all the crap away. Okay?"

"Okay."

"What are you doing tonight?"

"Learning lines."

"Tomorrow?"

"The same. It's six-thirty calls all week."

"You're not working Saturday."

"No."

"How about Friday night? I'll take you to my special restaurant. Wear some jeans so you're comfortable."

A tape recorder, a selection of tapes and a bunch of roses were delivered to her dressing room the following day. They were neatly labelled, "This is for grey days", "This is for calming you down". There were parts of symphonies, blues and rhythm music and one of his own electronic compositions on which he had written "This is for your soul". The high, delicate sounds lifted her spirit so that she rejoiced at the gift of survival. She shared her thoughts each night with a diary for Vladimir. A card from him was on her bedside table. It simply said "Learn to pray from the heart."

Mike didn't possess a car. He preferred to walk. Sophie shuffled along the pavements trying to keep pace with his steady stride. It was a warm April. They passed tourists strolling through Hyde Park and headed towards Berkeley Square where the trees were alive with the movements of birds.

"I played as a musician just up there in the Blue Angel nightclub."

Sophie's calves were aching. She couldn't remember when she had walked so far. They crossed Bond Street.

"And there in Churchills and up there in Winstons."

He guided her by either lightly touching her on the shoulder or by taking her gently by the hand. His palm was always dry, clean and smooth. It reminded her of her father's when, as a child, he would take her up West. But Mike had long tapering fingers, unlike Bill Rainbow's rough stubby ones.

They walked through the dirty streets of Soho where the air was filled with the sounds of restaurants and pop music to Tottenham Court Road. Down in a basement was a world of brass, incense and tantalising smells of spices.

"This is a vegetarian restaurant for very religious Hindus. You are about to discover your palate," Mike promised her.

It was almost sensual ecstasy. Their mouths tingled from a confusion of honey sweetness and hot spices. Like children they became delirious with the enjoyment. The soft strains of the sitar in the background added headiness to their conversation which led from music to space travel and Apollo thirteen to philosophical speculation.

"You know Sophie there are Illuminati in the world."

Sophie looked at him. On his ear lobes there was soft down. She would like to have touched but she paid attention to the conversation.

"These masters are on a higher vibratory level than us. They live in Tibet."

"Why?"

"Why what?"

"Why do they live in Tibet?"

"It's something to do with the remoteness, the inaccessibility, the air. I'll lend you a book."

"Are they Chinese?"

"No they're not physical like that. You can only see them if

96

you purify yourself. No meat, nicotine, alcohol. You have to prepare yourself."

"Mmm."

It was like being told a lovely fairy story. They wandered back to Chelsea, Mike expounding on his theories and Sophie aware of the warmth and touch of his arm. Since her divorce she had denied the feelings and emotions that were now cautiously unravelling and spreading with each movement of his hand. She was still frightened of rejection. He hugged her briefly outside Nell Gwynn House. She had shared his imaginary world, floated in his dreams but he was not invading her space. She wondered whether she was in love.

The next day he continued to weave a cocoon of magic around her. They walked across Hyde Park, passing brave sunbathers, courting couples and shouting children. He talked about rays, energies and the symbolic meanings of names. Sophie felt that her mind had been prised open ready to receive some wonderful secret.

His studio was a large attic in an old peeling house in the King's Road close to World's End. They sat on large bean bags, listened to music and drank tea made with cardamom seeds and honey. Dusk came and he put on tapes of his own electronic music.

"Let's meditate together." He lit a candle and placed it on the floor between them. "Think of love, Sophie. Let's try love."

She took the vibrations from his eyes. Incense perfumed the room. The suppressed sexual urge uncoiled through her spine until her cheeks flushed. He observed the change in her skin and closed his eyes.

"Shut your eyes and see your own universe Sophie."

The music caused her scalp to tingle. She soared into a starry cosmos where each galaxy centred around amber eyes. It was pure spiritual communion and time was measured by music. She sensed the candle splutter and saw the tears glinting on his cheekbones then tasted the salt from her own.

"This is what it's all about babe."

"Mmm."

"Nothing else."

She took a high dive into love. Days flew by. She laughed more, work became effortless and she bubbled through scene after scene.

"What are you on girl?" Hank asked.

"Life Hank, it's good."

She was on a spiritual honeymoon, drifting on a pink cloud of heightened sensations. They went to concerts together and sailed on imaginary journeys to a world of Tibetan masters, Eastern mountaintops and human perfection.

When Gloria telephoned to say that she and Steve were arriving for a long week-end at the Ritz, Sophie's life seemed complete.

Chapter Six

Gloria perched on the large bathtub and gazed round the surrounding marble walls. Her spoils from Fortnum and Mason's were scattered along the vanity unit. She picked up one of the lipsticks. One stroke of colour, a spray of Jungle Gardenia, a pat of her Vidal Sassoon haircut and she was a fashionable woman again. In the bedroom she collected her bag from under a pile of new tights, french brassières, scarves and silk panties and took a last glance at her reflection in the mirror. The Gucci suit looked swell.

The small lift dropped her by the Arlington Street entrance where she watched anxiously for Steve. He'd gone to buy some shirts from Jermyn Street. That had been almost an hour ago.

The hall porter approached her.

"Your husband's gone up the stairs to your suite, Mrs O'Connell."

"When he comes down, tell him I'm in the Palm Court will you?"

"Certainly Mrs O'Connell."

She walked along the corridor to the Piccadilly entrance where Sophie was expected to arrive then backtracked to hover on the steps of the Palm Court where she looked for the Irish guy in charge. He was from Cork. She had introduced herself to him when she reserved the table. She became nervous. Already the pink velvet chairs were being claimed for tea at the Ritz. Where the hell was Steve?

"Would you like to sit at your table, Mrs O'Connell and I'll look out for Miss Smith for you."

Michael Twomey, speaking in his soft Cork accent, led her discreetly to her table. He supervised the calm, polite atmosphere of the famous Palm Court and was noted for his tact with eccentric guests. He seated her well away from the potted palm, having noticed that she was inclined to bump into things. He lingered awhile, talking to the nervous woman until he saw her husband approach. He was a quiet sort of American, he thought. He saw the new Turnbull and Asser shirt and enquired whether Mr O'Connell was enjoying his visit.

Sophie had been to the Connaught, Claridges, the Savoy, most good hotels in London, but she had never been to the Ritz. The whole atmosphere was of slightly shabby gentility. The marble pillars and gilt were dull and the waiters' suits and the upholstery were worn and faded. She could see through to the Palm Court where a marble fountain was placed like an altar in a strange baroque church.

Michael Twomey escorted her past interested glances to Gloria and Steve's table. A well known gossip columnist waved. Gloria saw Sophie acknowledge him and felt proud. Everyone noticed Sophie's arrival.

The two women fell on each other, devouring one another's news, thrilled to be together. Steve volunteered the occasional remark when one of them paused for breath. The atmosphere became one of delirious madness.

Deft waiters carefully laid out some fine china. A choice of Indian or China tea was offered then salvers of delicate, assorted sandwiches arrived. Sophie observed the ritual reverently, trying the cream cheese first, then the cucumber and then working her way through the selection. Even Gloria stopped talking and sampled the tiny egg fingers. Steve picked out his favourite smoked salmon ones and the rest of the tea came in well timed stages. Scones, cream and jam and delicious small cakes.

"I've never had such a tea," said Sophie gathering the last of the crumbs. "What a wonderful place."

"Do you know what we ought to do Steve?" Gloria puffed a cigarette thoughtfully.

"No, but you're going to tell me."

"How about if we had our birthday here every year?"

"What, a joint fish birthday?" Sophie suggested.

"Yeh, we could get them to do a fish cake. We could have a different fish every year. What do you think Steve?"

"I think it's a great idea."

They called Michael over and explained their ideas to him. He liked the unusual request and assured them that it could be arranged. He walked away smiling at the caprices of the rich.

After tea they retired to the suite where Gloria showed Sophie all her new make-up. Steve sat reading in the lounge, listening to the continuous chatter coming from the bathroom. It was good to hear Gloria laughing so much, he thought. Sophie really was good for her. During the past few weeks, Steve had been troubled by Gloria's restlessness. He knew the signs from countless times in the past. The constant references to being uptight about something or other. He suspected that she needed the company of younger people like Sophie. Before Gloria arrived in Ireland he had made some good friends, kind people who had helped him during the lonely times without her. Unfortunately they were all in his own age group and Gloria's references to the women were growing ruder after each meeting. The men she declared to be boring arseholes.

He had asked around and found out that a lot of the Dublin

swingers, theatrical and society people were involved in charity work. Horse riding was the common sport for all people in Ireland. Between the charities and the riding, there had to be some way of introducing her to a new circle of friends. He kept meaning to get round to it. His other source of worry was highlighted when they arrived in London. Gloria always became randy in hotels and he just had to face the truth that he couldn't perform as often as he could in the past. Last night he had been so tired after the journey that he couldn't even get one erection. She had been okay about it but it distressed him. However, Sophie's presence had changed the whole mood between them. It was like it used to be. He ordered a whisky sour and some Coca-Cola for the girls from room service and relaxed while their giggles and murmurs continued from the bathroom.

Sophie was reorganising Gloria's make-up, showing her the modern way and steering her away from the old fashioned Lana Turner style. Gloria wanted to know more about Mike.

"Well he's special. You'll love him." Sophie tried to ex-plain about the music and the meditation but faltered with Gloria's total incomprehension.

"Bring him to dinner tomorrow. Steve . . ." she shouted.

"Yes dear?"

"Can you organise a table here for dinner tomorrow. Sophie's going to bring her new beau. Try and get table twenty-nine."

"Sure."

"Is he good in the sack?"

Sophie recoiled. For a split second Gloria sounded like Maggie. She began to stutter.

"Well, it's not like that."

"You mean you haven't?"

"No . . . It's not that kind of . . ." Sophie concentrated on the make-up and tried to divert Gloria from the subject. Gloria felt the distance between them and felt ashamed about her insensitivity. It had never affected her but she knew from the units that some alcoholics, especially the men, had difficulty adjusting to sex without the booze. She started to admire herself and the new make-up.

"Gee this is so much better. I look younger, don't I?" She studied herself closely through her glasses and watched out of the corner of her eye as Sophie's mood changed.

"Have you ever thought of contact lenses, Gloria?"

"No."

"You've got lovely eyes and hardly anyone ever sees them."

Gloria was overcome with emotion.

"You're the first gal who ever helped me look better. Most women don't give a damn or they're just plain mean about helping another dame."

Sophie hugged her. Gloria's face looked so tiny surrounded by tissue tucked into her neck.

"It's so good to see you. I don't think anyone makes me feel so . . ." She searched for words. "You know, like I belong."

Gloria had briefly felt usurped by the new guy in Sophie's life. Now she smiled, secure in the knowledge that their relationship was special.

"What's Hank Schwartz like?"

They gossiped about the film and the stars at Shepperton. Gloria felt part of the action again. She hung on to every word that Sophie told her. They talked until Sophie was dizzy with tiredness. She had been up since five o'clock in the morning. Now it was almost eight. Steve was making decisions for the evening. The combined smells of cigarette smoke and Jungle Gardenia filled the room and Sophie felt an urgent need for air.

"Shall I come round at about twelve for coffee? I'm going to Harrods first thing." Gloria was wide awake.

Steve sighed. "Let her sleep late tomorrow Mouse, she's pooped."

Gloria was contrite.

"I just can't wait to see your apartment. Will two o'clock be better?"

"Come at one and we'll take it from there, okay?"

Steve listened to their plans. With luck he would have all morning to himself. Perhaps he would go down to Fleet Street and see some of the guys at El Vino's.

Sophie strode along Piccadilly. When she walked she felt closer to Mike. Her pace increased and she swung her bag in rhythm with her step. Whenever she thought about him, music sounded inside her head. She was dying for Steve and Gloria to meet him. He had already met Jacob and Henry and they both approved.

"Very nice dear and he's not married?"

"No."

The air was becoming warmer and softer. Every cell in her body was awake to the approaching summer.

Gloria arrived promptly at one. She was laden with parcels and found it difficult to negotiate Sophie's tiny entrance hall. She explored the compact bathroom and kitchen recess, surprised that the apartment was so small. One lounge wall was made up of mirrors that gave an illusion of space. The other walls were shuttered cupboards and shelves.

"Where's the bedroom?"

Sophie laughed. "Here."

She pulled a bed out of a wall.

"Well, what about that. Gee that is really neat." Gloria paced the small floor area. "But dear, where do you entertain? I mean as an actress you have to entertain all those . . ."

"No I don't. I can get three or four people in here for coffee or I take them across to Luigi's, across the road."

"But what about the press?"

"I meet them out somewhere. I only allow close friends in here."

"Has Mike been here?"

"A couple of times."

They lunched at Luigi's. On her travels Sophie had learned enough Italian to exchange restaurant banalities. Gloria preened with all the attention they received from the management and waiters. Several men at other tables looked in their direction so she took out her new Dunhill lighter and lit a cigarette, watching carefully for any interested looks. Sure enough there was a speculative glance from a fellow on the corner table. Her ego satisfied, Gloria turned her attention to Sophie, probing her carefully about Mike.

"Dear, I hope you don't mind me asking but you know we're so emotionally vulnerable when we first come off the booze. Are you on the pill? I mean, I'd hate you to get yourself into trouble."

"No I'm not. It's not that kind . . . Don't worry, I can take care of myself. He's not the type . . ."

"They're all the type darling and you're a very beautiful girl. I just don't want you hurt."

"You'll love him Gloria, I promise."

They did look perfect together when they walked into the Rivoli Bar. Steve got up to welcome them. Gloria watched them approach. Sophie was flushing like a sixteen-year-old.

"Hi." Gloria shook hands with Mike.

"I've heard so much about you from Sophie," she said.

It was a neon light of recognition. She knew that he either had been or was still a user. Her protective mother instinct for Sophie quelled her natural exhibitionism so that she became like a skilled agent, inserting into the conversation coded words for him to understand and to reassure her that he was off it. Sophie and Steve were unaware of the undercurrent of tension. They all walked to the restaurant where the manager greeted them and led them to their table.

Mike didn't smoke. That was a good sign. He didn't drink and he was educated. Gloria scrutinised his appearance. His clothes were expensively casual. She joined in the conversation informing them that Rita Hayworth and Jackie Kennedy had once stayed at the Ritz and that she had been at the same school as Jackie Kennedy. Steve started dropping a few Hollywood names and told the story of the famous composer, who when asked on a chat show why he was so lucky said, "Isn't it funny, the harder I work, the luckier I get." Gloria listened to him telling all his favourite stories, and watched Mike's reactions. She was wondering what it was about him that worried her. He had assured her in code that he was off it. He was charming, gentle and hadn't put a foot wrong, so what was it that bothered her?

Mike dabbed his mouth with the starched napkin and smiled at her and Gloria remembered another mouth with the same weak sweetness. He jumped from a window on the sixty-fourth floor.

"Tom," she groaned.

"What dear?"

"Aah, bunged nose." She fumbled in her bag. Steve reached inside his pocket for some folded tissues.

Sophie ate sparingly. When she was with Mike she did not need to gorge her food. Unlike Gloria who smoked between mouthfuls, she was able to wait without anxiety for coffee before smoking. She knew that Steve and Gloria liked Mike and she was happy. She listened to him joking with Steve about his small experience of National Service in Malaya. This was the cue Steve needed for launching into stories of his own war.

"What part of the army were you in?" Gloria asked Mike.
"Intelligence."

"I suppose numbers and music go together." She blew her nose.

They all laughed. Gloria was surprised. She thought that she had said something profound.

Mike suggested going on to Ronnie Scott's jazz club. Steve was willing and Gloria was raring to go.

"Let's make a night of it. Let's go on afterwards to Annabel's."

Mike and Sophie's energy had given her the much needed lift from premature ageing that she had felt in Ireland. She wanted to recapture her youth, mix with the young and hear more new ideas. Steve's middle-aged, respectable friends were like vampires, draining her life's energy.

Steve remembered his jiving but tired quickly. Gloria sat and watched Sophie and Mike dancing wildly together. She looked around the crowded club and laughed.

"What is it Mouse?"

"Not one goddam homemade sweater in the place."

"Is that so."

She danced with Mike, apologising for being tone deaf and slightly off rhythm. He was so easy going that she started talking about her past addiction and emphasising her concern for Sophie. He was honest about himself and reassured her. "Cool it, cool it Gloria. I'm off H and I'm off shit. There is no way I would do anything to hurt Sophie. She's safe with me."

Most of her reservations about him vanished and she laughed and joked with him for the rest of the night.

It was Steve who called an end to the revels. He was tired, Annabel's was noisy and he wanted his slippers. He walked back to the Ritz arm in arm with Sophie.

"You really are great with Gloria. This trip has done her a lot of good."

He was impressed by the change in Sophie. Her face was alive and happy. He looked across to Gloria ranting away at Mike.

"Have you time to have tea tomorrow? I think we're having lunch with one of Gloria's mother's friends. Some Lady Something or other."

"What, here at the Ritz or do you want to come to my place?"

"No, come to the Ritz. We're not checking out till six and you don't want the bother."

"See you then Steve." She hugged him. His shoulders seemed to have become smaller and he had dark shadows under the eyes.

"Do you like them?" she asked Mike as they walked past Green Park.

The dry palm nursed her fluttering hand.

"They're two beautiful odd balls and they adore you, so I like them."

She nestled into his shoulder.

"I love Gloria. You know, I owe her my life."

They walked silently back to Nell Gwynn House.

"You are where you are." He held her and smoothed her damp hair. "And you are what you are because you have soul, Sophie." He kissed her forehead. "You bring out the best in me. I'm a much better person when I'm with you. But . . ." He sighed and shook his head.

Sophie looked into his eyes and wondered what caused the deep sadness. Was it the memory of his girlfriend, the singer? She stood on her toes and kissed his eyelids. The soft skin flinched and he eased away from her.

"You're one in a million," he said and smiled ruefully.

She wanted to reach out to him again but he was fighting some hidden conflict. He kissed her hand and she watched him amble along the deserted avenue. She wanted to cry out

108

"I love you Mike" but she was scared of losing his friendship. He reached Anderson Street and turned and waved.

Back at the Ritz Gloria was feeling dissatisfied. Steve had eaten too much and had wind. The electricity between Mike and Sophie had turned her on. When she had been with them, the air had tingled and she had been lifted to a heightened state and she didn't want to come down. Steve was in the bathroom farting and cleaning his dental plate. She wanted to shake him for killing the romance.

The following afternoon, over tea, Gloria complained about the boredom of life in Ireland.

"Have you ever worked, Gloria?" Sophie asked.

"Why dear?"

"Well, why don't you get a job? I think your brain's too good to be sitting around all day doing nothing."

"Funny dear, I wrote a feature page when we were poor. About famous people's jewellery."

"It was hardly a feature page Gloria," Steve said. "You just gave us the names for the pictures and the caption writers did the rest."

Gloria looked deflated.

"Would you like to write Gloria?" Sophie asked, glaring at Steve.

"Well," Gloria paused and looked at Steve. "As a matter of fact, I have thought about it. I'd like to write about the dogs. 'Lottie goes to Ireland'. You know the sort of thing." She warmed to the idea. "I think I could try a kinda Thurber."

"Let your mind alone." Steve started to laugh.

Sophie ignored him. "You mean a children's book?"

"Yeah, for sophisticated kids," Gloria said. She became inspired. "I could get someone to do the drawings. Hey Steve, I could write a kid's book. Do you think I could?"

"Sure, why not?"

Gloria became excited and announced that she would

dedicate the book to Steve and Sophie. Steve promised that he would type up her manuscript.

They dropped Sophie off on the way to the airport.

"When you've finished the film, come and have a holiday with us. And bring Mike."

"I'll do that."

It was a warm evening. Sophie gazed up at the still blue sky. Gloria was like a whirlwind, churning up her memories and lifting her self-confidence. She thought of the conversations during the past few days and found herself laughing out loud. She remembered Vladimir and the fact that she hadn't written for a couple of weeks. There was so much to tell him about Mike's theories and stories.

As she wrote to the old priest she found herself crying. So much had happened so quickly. She had been given an overdose of happiness and the voice of the old self-destructive Sophie from the past whispered pessimistic fears. Gloria had emphasised that she should live each day at a time but it was hard not to hope for the fantasies that she entertained when she was with Mike. Gloria and Steve had promised her an eternity of tea at the Ritz but life wasn't like that.

There was a niggling sense of shame that she had failed to visit her mother since her return from Dublin. All the meditation, masters and glamorous teas had not given her the courage to face that squalid reality.

She shared all her thoughts with Vladimir. His reply arrived by return post. A parcel contained a bible and a letter.

"My dearest Sophie,

You will find all your answers in this book. It is good to meditate on all God's work. Numbers and symbols are part of a significant design. You do not have to travel to Tibet to find the mountain that is within yourself. Neither do you have to find strange beings to learn about spirituality. Study the lives of saints who struggled with their human weaknesses. Failure, dear Sophie, is one way of ridding ourselves of pride. So always thank God for your failures. Christ will enter your heart with prayer. He loves us with all our imperfections, so who are we to demand perfection in others."

The rest of the letter contained news about Dublin and his garden. She could almost feel the peacefulness of his sitting room. She kept the letter in the bible, reading it each day. The words were an anchor for her turbulent thoughts.

Chapter Seven

The charity ball was held in a large country house in Wicklow. The invitations were the result of Steve's large donation which he considered to be a good investment towards future harmony in the home.

In her green dress from Harrods, wearing new make-up and with the extra confidence from contact lenses, Gloria was certain of a personal social triumph.

She and Steve mingled with the other guests, many of whom were discussing the impending British elections and the cancelled South African cricket tour. There was talk of horses and gossip about people whose names were familiar to Steve but of whom she knew nothing. The waves of dissatisfaction washed over her. She longed for the youthful exuberance associated with Mike and Sophie's company.

It was a fraction of a moment, when boredom had isolated her from the conversation, that she spotted them. They stood in the corner of the room under a large ancestral portrait, their backs to the dancing, noisy crowd. The silent brotherhood attracted the lapsed member. She drifted towards them. They were slower in their movements and quieter in their conversation. Their body language confirmed her intuition. They turned as she approached them. Some were drinking orange juice, others were rolling their cigarettes. From packets of Marlborough came the glint of aluminium foil.

"Hi."

She was like a homing pigeon back with her own kind. It was easier. There was automatic acceptance and a guaranteed network of social contact. One of the girls was an air hostess, another the son of an influential Dublin politician. Dermot, with the long, flowing hair, was an artist and the others were an assortment of writers, students and landowners.

Steve saw her laughing with the younger set and turned back to his friend who was arranging some shark fishing in Cork. While they swopped stories about the ones that got away, Gloria filled her evening bag with precious future moments and smoked her first joint for almost six months. Her brain became clear and divided into compartments. Colours intensified and she heard every syllable of humour. She laughed until her cheeks ached. Eventually she floated back to Steve, waltzed with his friends from Cork and talked a lot about her ideas for her book.

Her study was arranged at the top of the house. Armed with notepad and pencil, she sat planning her book. The windows were kept open. She assured Steve that incense was inspiring and after her ration of two joints she liberally sprayed the room with Jungle Gardenia. Calm detachment was what she needed if she was to write the book, she decided, and that was only possible with pot. After all, her life was now full of charity meetings, hairdresser's appointments and late-night entertaining. Dermot and his friends regularly dropped in at night for coffee or tea and to give her a fresh supply. She bought one of Dermot's paintings. It was a mixture of red and orange patterns called "Dublin at Night". Steve would join them for a while but then retire to bed, leaving them to talk until three in the morning. Gloria felt popular and part of a youthful existence. She phoned Sophie to tell her about her friends and when Sophie asked whether she was feeling all right, the warning bell sounded, so she confessed to slight 'flu and made a mental note to cut down the marijuana.

Steve felt a great weariness. There was nothing he could do when she started the deception. He understood the attraction for her new friends. The pattern had recurred throughout their married life. He couldn't fight it again, he just didn't have the energy. All he could do was to keep her occupied and to delay the inevitable grand slam. He confronted her with the truth but she assured him that this time she could handle it and quoted a list of celebrities who used it occasionally. It was pointless to argue, she would only begin to hide it. At least when she was being half truthful, he could monitor her habit. Also troubling him was his apparent impotence. He was terrified that she might take a lover. At least with pot and her scribbling she was content with sex play and sleep.

Security was all she needed and he could always give her a cuddle. When Maureen, the cook, was around he had a hard on. Sometimes he entertained fantasies about her, especially when she was bending over the oven. It was something to do with the neat apron and her pretty legs. He had paid her a few compliments but she had ignored them. He didn't want to press her any further in case he was left with Mary and her stews.

He managed to get Gloria away for a weekend fishing in Kinsale. The change of air agreed with her and she was in great form, entertaining everyone with her stories about the dogs. But Dermot became involved with the book too, by offering to draw the illustrations. Steve smoked some grass with them all one night in an attempt to be part of the strange world but it did nothing for him except make him wheezy and thirsty. For a moment though he did not feel such an outsider.

He had heard that a lot of people were trying Tunisia for their holidays. It sounded the perfect place to take her and it would break the routine of her pot-smoking sessions.

Perhaps he should wait for Sophie to finish her film and ask her to come with them. Gloria would behave while she was around. She was so protective about the girl that she would not set a bad example. Steve plotted and schemed and found out about hotels.

*

By chance, Sophie was not needed at the studios on June the fourth. She stood in Paddington Station waiting apprehensively for the Plymouth train to arrive and moved her position whenever she felt curious glances from waiting passengers. Despite the hot weather she had goosepimples on her bare arms. She listened to the sounds of departing trains, blurred announcements and running feet, and wondered whether she would recognise him. Once before when he had returned from prison she had been confronted with a stranger. She walked back to the platform and stood shuffling her feet, looking up to the dirty iron arches and smutty skylights.

She had gone round to her mother's place in Foskett Road and told her that she would be meeting her father. After an hour, the cloying smell of wallflower room spray, the frustration of listening to the nagging whine and petty resentments, made her feel sick and faint. Every nerve in her body screamed when she touched the clammy cheeks and inhaled the warm, stale hair lacquer.

"Don't look at me like that."

"I'm not looking like anything."

"Bloody lady muck."

"Why don't you open the windows? It's so hot in here."

"Because there'd be a draught. You wait till you get arthritis and your bones ache."

"You'd feel better if you let some air in or sat outside in the sun."

"And how do I manage on these knees?"

"Perhaps if you could diet a bit, it would ease the pressure."

The row began. Insults were hurled around the stuffy room.

She felt a moment of compassion for the fat unhappy woman, but years of childhood rejection were hard to forget. She left with relief, the vicious messages for Bill Rainbow ringing in her ears.

She recognised him instantly. His gaunt figure attempted a jaunty walk along the platform. The effect was almost grotesque. His effort at nonchalance brought tears to her eyes. He noticed the wetness of her cheeks and his mouth wobbled in sympathy. He fought hard and gave a twisted smile.

"Hello Sophie."

"Dad."

They walked in silence to the taxi rank.

"How's your Mum?"

"Okay."

She had found him a small flat in Pimlico. As the taxi turned into Winchester Street, bells chimed from the Catholic church opposite the row of shabby houses. Sophie made him some tea while he unpacked. She could hear the muffled sniffs as he opened and shut drawers.

"Are you sure you don't want a sandwich?"

"No, I had enough on the train."

"This friend says we can have the flat for six months. He's gone on tour to America."

"You were in Ireland weren't you?"

"Yes."

"Dartmoor was built to put the IRA in, you know."

"Was it?"

"Meet any of them when you was filming, did you?"

"Don't think so."

"Don't suppose you would, not with your life."

He paced the room. Outside in the street some Italians were shouting at each other.

"One of your films was shown last year. I didn't let on of course. It was funny sitting watching. You were a lot younger."

He wanted to walk. They went down to the river and crossed Vauxhall Bridge.

"Do you like Chinese food Dad?"

"Never had it."

"Would you like to go to a Chinese restaurant tonight?"

"What's it like then? Don't eat snails and things, do they?"

"No, I think you'd like it."

Later she watched him cautiously eating sweet and sour prawns and wondered at the reversal of their roles. When she had been a child it had always been Dad who had taken her to the zoo or to watch the changing of the guard. Maggie's role had been to serve food reluctantly, considering it her only maternal duty.

"What do you think you'll do, Dad?"

"Well, there's this bloke who's got some places in Soho. I knew him in the army."

"What sort of places?"

"Don't worry love. I'm never going back inside again."

She showed him where she lived and he started to laugh. She loved the sound.

"I used to know a couple of toms who worked a beat round here. One of them was called Maisie. Good-natured tarts they were."

"Really."

"Yeah, they were alibis for a couple of lads on the cinema job. The old bill never did get them." He couldn't stop laughing.

He obviously never knew about Maggie, Sophie thought. It

was only she who knew and that was because she had followed her one night wanting to know where Mum was going just before Christmas. She had been full of eight-year-old excitement wondering whether Maggie had found a second-hand doll's pram and was going to collect it. She had shadowed her through the streets, seen her join the group of overmade up women and watched as a man approached her. Sophie pushed the memory back.

Before he left she gave him an envelope.

"To tide you over, Dad."

"I'll try to make it up to you Sophie, I promise."

"No need."

He hugged her and they both cried.

*

Steve read through all the spelling mistakes and rambling narrative. It was awful, no publisher would touch it, but at least it was keeping her occupied. It was a love story between a dachshund and a mongrel. He was the mongrel.

Gloria sat watching his responses. She had her writer's outfit on, an Elle trouser suit with a biro dangling on a gilt chain.

"It's coming on Mouse." She looked so little and vulnerable. He had to reassure her that her efforts had been worthwhile.

"Would you put the commas and full-stops in and type it for me Steve?"

"Sure."

"And you really think it's good?"

"It's certainly got something."

Each afternoon she would disappear to the top of the house with her notepad. Then the windows would open and he knew she was smoking pot. The story had changed over the weeks. There was a puppy which was obviously Sophie and a number of other dogs. Each chapter revealed a growing confusion in Gloria's mind. But the puppy and the mongrel were still important to the dachshund. Until that situation changed, he knew the drugs were still under control.

"Do you like Dermot's illustrations?"

"Sure. Stick with it Mouse, you're doing great."

*

Saturday was a perfect day starting with a lunchtime party aboard a boat moored on the Thames. It was given by Sophie's father's friend, and now employer, Julian.

"Bill's told me about his famous daughter. He's very proud of you Sophie."

Julian Castellucci spoke in a soft American accent. According to Bill, Julian ran casinos and had other interests. Sophie was cautious of the smoothly polite man. She had met similar people connected to the film business, usually the anonymous backers who occasionally turned up on a set but were never introduced. But she felt grateful to him for Bill's new confidence. Julian had given him a job and treated him with respect. She watched as a woman gently flirted with her father. He was wearing a very smart new suit, his face was tanned and he had lost the haunted look in his eyes. He caught sight of her observing him and looked embarrassed. Sophie decided it was time to leave. She didn't want to cramp his style and she had a lot of lines to learn for the following Monday. Bill escorted her to a taxi and pressed an envelope into her hand. He was returning the loan, he said. He emphasised the word loan so that Sophie didn't contradict him.

"Be careful, Dad."

"Sophie, I'm so legal, believe me. Julian is a business man. I'm paying stamps and the lot."

She could smell his aftershave on her hand as she drove home in the cab.

The radio announcement said that it was the hottest day for a century. All along Sloane Avenue windows were open and Sophie could hear people's conversations as they prepared supper. She learnt the lines quicker than she expected and felt that she wanted to run and join the people in the streets celebrating Saturday night. From the radio came the haunting strains of Siegfried's Idyll and she thought of Mike. She wanted to touch his soft brown hair and kiss the gentle amber eyes. She hadn't seen him for a couple of days and felt an urgent desire to be with him. Sometimes she felt confused about her feelings. Part of her loved him for never having made a pass but often she was puzzled and disappointed by his restraint.

She looked out of the window wishing she could see him walking up the street. Groups and couples walked towards the King's Road. She decided to call round and surprise him. She had found a small Chinese water-colour which she knew he would love. She wrapped it carefully and enclosed a card then put on a fresh summer dress and sprayed herself with Joy. Her skin, already pink from the morning on the river, flushed with a sense of anticipation. She walked through the streets with echoes of Wagner ringing in her head.

She ran up the stairs two at a time shouting his name. The door on the landing was ajar and she rushed through. The atmosphere of hot sheets and sweat hit her. Mike had managed to pull a duvet over his body but the woman lay nude and unashamed. Sophie recognised the sensual face from a photograph Mike had shown her.

Stammering with embarrassment, and hot with shame, Sophie backed out of the door. She left the water-colour on the landing and fled. Once home, shivering with emptiness, she turned on her music to muffle her animal-like howls.

Exhausted, she sat listening to the sounds in the street and trying to pray like Vladimir had taught her.

"Why?" she whispered.

"Whoever you are, whatever you are, please help me."

The telephone rang seconds later. It was Gloria.

Once again Gloria crooned and mothered Sophie out of her misery.

"Sophie, when do you finish the filming?"

"Next Tuesday if all goes well."

"Steve and I are going to Tunisia for a holiday. It would be great if you could come with us."

Sophie lay in the darkness listening to her own heart beat. The room seemed charged with electric silence. She wondered whether the phone call had been a coincidence or whether some unseen power had answered her prayer.

Chapter Eight

His battered straw hat half covered the old man's lined, dignified face. Waiters in brightly coloured shirts called to him on their way to the restaurant. They enquired about his family, commented on their day or shared a joke. All day, the old man gathered up used towels and moved mattresses for the guests. Occasionally, he stopped, sat in the shade and watched the Europeans burning their skin. He saw Sophie pick up her towels and walk past Steve who was under a parasol reading a thriller. He heard her call to Gloria who was in the pool bar drinking coffee with some Italians.

"I'm going into the sea. See you later."

The old man padded across the sun terrace and removed her mattress.

Gloria waited a few minutes and then followed Sophie along the shaded path towards the beach. She saw the lifeguard perched on his platform. As Sophie passed him, the young Arab turned his head in her direction. Gloria relaxed. She had paid the young man to keep a special eye on Sophie when she swam alone. The haunting memory of Meg had returned when Sophie first plunged into the sea and stayed underneath for what seemed like hours. Gloria had run screaming to the lifeguard to save her, only to be shown the arms flashing through the water. It was then she had made her deal with him.

Sophie floated on the water, her face worshipping the

hot North African sun. The sea around her was like a vast, moving prism of light. She drifted like a grain of salt dissolving into the warm caressing waves.

On the night flight over to join Steve and Gloria she had decided to switch off her mind and concentrate only on bodily sensation. The strange power that had answered her prayer with a holiday in Tunisia seemed intent on proving it was still around. Picking up a newspaper on the plane, she saw the headline HARLEY STREET DOCTOR SENT TO JAIL. Stoller's past had caught up with him. Luckily she had a row of seats to herself so her loud whispering to the Power could not be overheard. "Okay," she had hissed, "I know you're there but don't for Christ's sake turn up in a burning bush or anything until I'm on the ground."

Gloria had met her at the airport and mistaken her glazed expression for grief and held her hand all the way to the hotel. They had driven through dark, country roads with Sophie deciding that as love hurt and emotion could lead to delusion, she was putting herself into neutral and switching off her mind.

Small fish tickled her feet. She let herself drift towards the shore. The waves pushed her on to the beach where she lay like a starfish, the waves lapping round her legs.

"Sind Sie Deutsch?"

A middle-aged man looked down at her. He had a thin scar on his chest.

"Nein. I'm English."

"Really? You do not look English."

"Oh."

"I love the English."

He sat down beside her and stretched his feet into the ebbing tide.

"I must be careful." He pointed to his chest. "Heart . . ."

"Ah."

"Is this your first time here?"

"Yes."

"I come every year."

"Oh."

"It was here I made a great change. You understand, I was a prisoner of the English."

Sophie sat up.

"Were you with Rommel?"

"Yes. The English officer, he never sat in the sun. He always wore uniform. Germans sit in the sun," he said.

Sophie laughed.

"But I was so young. I was glad to be a prisoner. We had no food or medicine. The English gave us food and medicine. I did not believe it. We were the enemy, yet they gave us food." The German stared hard at his feet.

"I must change everything I think. All my philosophy . . ." He paused. "I come here every year to remember."

Sophie was thinking about the old newsreels of marching Hitler Youth and trying to imagine the German lost in the desert.

"Mmm."

As if in answer to her thoughts the German went on. "I have a photograph here. When I was a young soldier. I can show you later."

They became silent—he remembering his youth, she pondering on the need to have an old snapshot on holiday.

A sailing boat dropped anchor and a shoal of pink-skinned Europeans swam out to it. Some on rubber mattresses paddled alongside them.

A muezzin called to the faithful. "God is most Great . . ."

Arabs from other countries became still like shadows on the sand.

Across the beach came the sound of a woman's voice. "Helmut. Komm bitte."

The German stood up. "My nurse. I must rest before evening."

He walked slowly towards a slim woman in a striped dress.

The carton was labelled Multi vitamins. Gloria shook a selection of barbiturates into her palm and made her choice. She looked at her reflection in the bathroom mirror. The hairdresser had done her hair well. It gleamed like a sunlit halo around her head. She pulled on an expensive new caftan bought from a boutique in Sousse and admired the dramatic effect.

Steve was snoring loudly on the bed. Gloria found the solid silver collar on the dressing table and eased it around her thin neck. The hand of Fatima dangled in front of her throat. She closed the door quietly and crept along the parapet between the apartments. She could see Sophie down by the water's edge, enjoying the last rays of the sun. The sand that by day had been trampled over by indifferent feet was now washed smooth.

She walked past hanging bougainvillaea and floodlit palm trees. The smell of jasmine hung in the air.

The manager was in the bar talking easily in either French, German or Italian. He spoke English with a slight American accent which Gloria liked to hear. He noticed her approach and broke away from the other guests.

"Good evening, Madam. You are on your own?"

"Aw, Steve's flat out on the bed."

"Will you have a drink with me?"

"I'd love to."

He only had to raise his voice and waiters leapt into action. Gloria liked his polite manner and admired his white suit. He helped her to a seat, gently brushing the inside of her arm with his soft fingers. There was a faint smell of musk on his skin.

They were served fruit cocktails dressed with slices of

orange. Gloria sipped cautiously. The night before she had dropped the orange straight into her lap.

"It is interesting." He removed the piece of orange.

"I find that European men become tired in the heat while the women become more . . ." He paused. "Energetic."

His eyes were like scissors cutting off her caftan. He moved his mouth sensually around the words so that every utterance was an invitation to bed. Gloria felt a lustful glow.

"Oh, Steve always gets energetic after breakfast. That's when he has his wind surfing lesson, of course."

"Yes, I forgot. He enjoys his lessons?"

"He sure does. He keeps at it for a whole hour. That's when I'm usually in the suite reading or writing notes."

He looked amused. "I walk past your rooms on the way for my bathe. Perhaps I should call upon you?"

"Why don't you do that?"

Sophie saw the manager talking to Gloria. He reminded her of a squat, smooth, music hall turn. She was about to join them when Gloria spotted her.

"Are you going to change, Sophie?"

She didn't want the younger girl breaking up the mood.

"Yes. I'm covered in sand. I'm really hungry."

"Will you wake up Steve on the way, dear?"

"All right."

Sophie walked through grounds vibrating with the sounds of crickets and frogs. Insects flew towards the lights concealed among bushes and branches. She hammered on Steve's door until he woke, then entered her own suite to find one of the hotel staff spraying her room with insect repellent. She waited patiently until he finished then opened all the shutters to remove the smell.

All sand and salt removed, she emerged from the steamy bathroom and went out on to the balcony.

The stars seemed larger in the Tunisian sky. Palm trees

rustled and murmured in tune with the sigh of the sea. Along the coastline, lights flickered from other hotels and beach bars. She felt her hair drying in the warm air and shook her head back to gaze at the heavens. It was natural to pray, to wish to be a part of the throbbing, individual energies that shone through the darkness. She whispered her respect to the unknown being. A large shooting star dropped across the sky.

The barbeque was spread out across the terrace. Sophie joined Steve and Gloria at their allotted table. Gloria was surrounded by some young Frenchmen. Sophie smiled. Her friend was in great form. Steve was relaxed and enjoying the party mood. Sophie couldn't cope with discussions about the result of Britain's elections again. She was ravenous, so headed for the couscous queue. Helmut was already there with his nurse. He reached into his pocket and pulled out a faded snapshot of a young German soldier with sad eyes.

"That was me, a young prisoner of war." He spoke lovingly as if referring to a son.

"You see how confused I look. A young man trying to free himself from the years of indoctrination by family and state."

Sophie touched the photograph reverently.

"It was in this country, not far from here, that I began my own life . . . I'm sorry but I do not know your name."

"Sophie."

"Sophie, I come here to honour my own evolution."

They moved closer to the table and helped themselves to food.

A young Frenchman attempted to flirt but Sophie was intent on chewing a chicken bone. Gloria watched her. The girl's skin was the shade of lightly done toast and her hair the colour of ripe corn. In many ways, she was like a child, Gloria thought. She had switched off from the trials of the adult world and was content just to roam the beaches and swim. She wondered whether Mike would have gone back to his ex-girlfriend if Sophie had gone to bed with him earlier in the relationship. Sophie looked up at her and grinned and Gloria's heart missed a beat. It was Meg's scrubbed innocence reappearing like a caul on Sophie's face.

"You are looking great tonight, Mouse," Steve whispered. She reacted coquettishly.

"You look like a real Hollywood star, don't you think so Sophie?"

"She is incredibly glamorous," Sophie agreed. "I love that caftan."

A small group of local musicians were discussing their programme and adjusting their seats.

"Well girls? Shall we go over and listen?" Steve placed a possessive hand on Gloria's shoulder.

The drum's incessant rhythm was joined by a tambourine and then the men began their chant, which was echoed by the wail of a violin. Sophie watched the shadows from the drummer's hands dancing on a wall. Gloria began talking to some people so she moved away to a chair closer to the players and avoided the distractions of drinks being served, change counted and fidgeting bodies.

She leant back in the soft chair and looked up at the stars, remembering all the concerts with Mike. The repetitive music became louder and quicker dispersing her wistfulness to the sky and filling her body with the throbbing sound. Almost mesmerised by the vast numbers of stars, she thought she could hear Vladimir's voice whispering through the rhythm.

"He gave you friendship and brotherly love. He broadened your interests, gave you music to fill the emptiness and altered your view of life. Why then, did you demand more than he could give?"

Sophie sat up and stared at the musicians, half expecting

Vladimir to be there with them. The young drummer smiled at her.

Poor Mike, she thought, how could he possibly have lived up to her fantasies. The Mike whom she had created had never existed. The gentle man who wanted to share his music and philosophies with someone in need, had only ever offered her friendship. He had always been honest about his past love. Sophie replayed past conversations in her mind. She had never really listened.

The music stopped. As well as applauding the music, Sophie clapped her own transformed sense of reality.

She heard Gloria talking loudly with some Italians and remembered how Mike had tried to dispense with words and communicate through music or by the silence of meditation. She thought of the German on the beach and his courage to change his attitude to life, to see the reality and reject a collective fantasy. She joined Gloria and listened to the almost feverish discussions about Bourguiba and Tunisia's future. Gloria's eyes were over-bright and she talked through other people's words. Sophie heard the silent cry through Gloria's babbling. It said, "Please love me, please think I'm intelligent, please don't find me boring and leave me alone." She bent down and whispered in her ear.

"I love you Gloria."

The older woman stopped mid-sentence and her eyes became as confused as those of a small child.

"And I love you too, darling," she said huskily.

A young boy dressed in a white jellabah and wearing a small white skull cap offered them garlands of jasmine. Steve bought them one each. "For my two fish." He placed them ceremonially around their necks.

The musicians were gathering up their instruments and preparing for departure when they were passed by new guests arriving from Europe. A pop group crashed into rhythm, the

Western music creating a harshness and destroying the gentle evening. Couples began to dance, their faces assuming frantic masks of abandon. The young singer gasped out a song, the veins in his neck straining to reach the unnatural sounds. Sophie couldn't cope with the change in mood.

She excused herself and left for the peace of her room.

She stood naked on the balcony, grateful for the gentle breeze. From the hotels along the beaches, more amplified music screeched irreverently to the sky. A confused cockerel crowed in reply. Sophie lit a candle and placed it on a table in the centre of the garland of jasmine and then attuned her ears to the steady sounds from nature—the rhythm from the sea, the whispered music through the trees and the softly spoken words from passing security guards. She remembered Helmut's words, "I come here to honour my own evolution", and looked back on her own development since she had first set foot in Dublin. It had been like a journey through awareness. People had come into her life like sign posts to new directions of thought. She wondered about her destination and looked up to the stars for an answer. All she could hear was Vladimir's voice say, "Sophie, learn to pray from the heart."

Months of early rising had made lying in bed impossible. In Tunisia, Sophie slept well and woke refreshed with the sounds of daybreak. It became a ritual to pay homage to the sun in the East, standing poised, breathing in the morning air until the rays became too strong to watch. Then she would wander down to the sea, marking the virgin sand with her footprints and plunge into the water.

Drifting with the tide, she listened to the camels complaining as the handlers brought them along the beach. Some were being prepared for a long trek with tourists dressed as Bedouins, others were settling sullenly into the sand, waiting for the monotonous routine of giving rides up and down familiar tracks.

She was always ready for breakfast and, snug in her towelling dressing gown, would watch all the different guests meander to their seats. The Germans were first down, followed by the Swiss, then the French and Italians. Steve would join her when she was drinking her second cup of coffee and the English would arrive just before breakfast was cleared away.

Gloria preferred to take coffee in her suite after which she would go back to bed, then rise at lunchtime to appear on the terrace in some beautiful outfit.

"Why don't you try wind surfing Sophie? It's not hard when you get the hang of it," Steve asked.

"I'm going to Nebeul this morning. I want to see the market. Do you think Gloria might like to come?"

"When does the coach leave?"

"At nine-thirty."

"She'd never make it. It would take her three hours to get ready."

"I'll ask her anyway."

Sophie thought she heard the sound of a kitten in distress and paused on the steps to the apartments to look up to the trees. The sounds came again. They seemed to be coming from Gloria's room. Sophie hurried in the direction of the mewling cries and was just about to knock on the door when she heard the man's voice and Gloria's laugh of pleasure. She froze. Along the parapet, a cleaner was collecting towels from the rooms and clanking a bucket. She greeted Sophie who returned a smile, then, indicating to the curious woman the DO NOT DISTURB notice on Gloria's door, tip-toed across to her own room.

From her balcony, Sophie could see Steve talking to the wind surfing coach. She dressed quickly, all the while

131

wondering who was in Gloria's room. She was concerned that she might run into whoever it was, so lingered awhile before leaving. She heard Gloria's door slam and peeped through the spyhole in her own door. She saw the squat legs walk towards the steps and then saw the manager's face turn to make sure that he had not been seen. Heart pounding, she waited until his steps died away, then quietly, she crossed the parapet and fled to the waiting coach.

Sophie watched the landscape go past feeling like an evacuee from security. Her childhood memories of Maggie's indiscretions returned to haunt her. Apart from her disappointment in Gloria, she was amazed at the woman's audacity. The risk taken when Steve could quite possibly have walked in on the act. She brooded, wondering whether to tell Gloria that she knew of the affair.

Perspiration trickled down her neck and flies attacked from all sides. She walked past piles of melons and stalls of clay pottery. On both sides of the street the tourists were asked to buy drums or leather goods. They passed rooms where men smoked from hookahs or sipped from small cups of black tea or coffee. Everywhere throbbed with the sound of voices offering their wares. The group was led through the market where many took photographs of camel traders with stained or missing teeth. Sophie wandered past piles of clothes and jewellery laid out in the bright sunshine, then through the market place towards a small shop selling art and precious stones. Some Germans were looking inside. She tagged behind, grateful to be out of the heat.

She had seen the amber rocks before, either in baskets or heaped on stalls with other tourist paraphernalia but she had never looked closely to see what they were.

In the small shop, each individual piece was carefully displayed. Sophie picked one up.

"English?"

"Yes."

The trader had a paler skin than his contemporaries. He was tall, dignified and his dark blue jellabah rustled as he walked towards her.

"These are very fine examples, don't you agree?"

"It's a sort of rose."

"Desert rose. Over many years the sand comes together to make such a rose."

Sophie lifted the jagged crystal up to her eyes and looked into the amber folds. It was like holding a part of the Sahara in her hand.

"I'll take two."

Gloria and Steve were sitting by the pool. Everything was so normal that Sophie wondered whether she had imagined the earlier incident.

"Hi Sophie, what did you think of Nebeul?"

She told them about the trip watching Gloria closely for any signs of guilt. There was none to be seen. If anything, Gloria was more relaxed than she had been before. Sophie presented her with the rose and explained its origins.

"Oh thank you, darling. Steve, don't you think this would make an unusual paperweight?"

"Yeah, very unusual. Looks like a kind of shell. Would you like a Coke Sophie?"

"No thanks. I'm so hot I think I'll have a swim."

"We're going to eat at the beach bar later. We'll see you down there."

It was stupid to feel so disappointed. She knew that Gloria did not see things in the same way but she felt a loneliness, a loss of trust. She couldn't share the important thoughts with her, only the very basic, emotional ones. It seemed that the only people with whom she could share any spiritual thoughts or philosophy were Vladimir or Mike.

She placed the rose on the balcony table and trickled some

water through the jagged petals, then watched it glinting in the sunlight. Sahara winds had breathed through the fine sand until the particles had clung together and formed this beautiful rose. She touched the fragile edges. Were humans created in the same way? Did a cosmic breath blow the fragile thoughts that formed a rose in the heart?

She returned to the sea, a lone fish, isolated from the laughter on the beach, only aware of the need to share her thoughts. To contemplate life gave an awareness of being but it was necessary to share to feel alive. She saw Helmut sitting by the water's edge and swam towards him. She had to hear some words of inspiration. It was as if her soul was starving.

He was pleased to have her company. He talked about the war years and his youth and she shared her thoughts about the rose and her occasional disappointment with people. The German listened patiently.

"Sometimes, Sophie, I think we have too much expectation of people. I am twice your age but it is a lesson I must always learn. I learned in my youth the dangers of worshipping a personality. Then I learned again through two marriages the same lesson—not to put all trust in personality, it leads to disappointment. Yet we cannot recognise the truth of another person until we have our own truth. Look at me. I was a soldier because it was expected of me but I was not happy as a soldier. I became a dentist, a rich dentist because I think that is what I should be, rich and successful. But I always wanted to sail a boat. That is what gives me my own self. I have now learned towards the end of my life that what I really needed, to be true to myself, was to be a fisherman."

Sophie listened to Gloria's conversation during lunch. There was so much to learn. She had first had to learn how to listen, now she had to try and understand. Perhaps in that way she could be a better friend to the older woman. She felt ashamed of her shallow friendship towards Gloria. Whenever she had been in trouble Gloria had been ready to help immediately, while she when faced with one of Gloria's problems had recoiled, disappointed that the older woman had not lived up to her high expectations.

Small boats rested on the beach, their rigging tinkling against the aluminium masts. Sophie perched inside one and watched Gloria paddling, her sarong lifted above her pale knees. The words had to be said. The trust found to share the secret.

"I know about the manager, Gloria." She blurted it out. "I heard you this morning."

Gloria continued to paddle, changing her direction into a circular movement. Sophie bit her nails and waited for a response.

"It's just that . . . well, you ought to be careful. What if Steve finds out?"

Gloria looked at Sophie's anxious face and felt old. Challenged by anyone else she would have sworn and spelt out explicitly the exact nature of her needs but Sophie was special. She did not want to either hurt or lose her respect and friendship. She joined her and climbed into the boat.

"How can I make you understand something that isn't important to you?" Gloria said.

Sophie ached to understand.

"I love Steve, Sophie, but I've just got to have sex. And he's a lot older than I am as you know and well . . . he just can't make it these days. He hasn't for a couple of months now. And I know it worries him to fail, so I don't bother him. But if I don't get a good screw, Jesus, I just don't exist. I really need it Sophie . . . to feel alive. I mean, Ibrahim means nothing to me. He's just there. If it wasn't him, it would be the first guy with a twinkle in his eye. I ask you, what harm does it do, Sophie? Ibrahim's happy, I feel great and Steve looks really macho on his windsurf."

"But what if he falls off?"

"What if who falls off what?"

Gloria started to laugh and Sophie joined in. From his deckchair Steve could see them hugging each other obviously delirious over some joke. He smiled. The holiday had been a good idea. Gloria's whole personality had improved. Sophie was a good influence on her. Perhaps he should extend the vacation for another week. He turned his attention back to the out-of-date newspaper to read about the tensions in Northern Ireland.

Sophie took up windsurfing for the remaining weeks in order to safeguard Gloria's illicit therapy. Steve enjoyed her company and took a delight in escorting her down to the beach each morning. As Gloria shared her thoughts and past exploits with her, Sophie found that she was beginning to understand her own mother. Male attention and sex were as important to some women as the security of friendship and the communion of spiritual ideas were to her. She and Gloria were two fish swimming in opposite directions, each heading for some truth dictated by their own natures.

Early in September, Sophie returned to Ireland with Gloria and Steve and stayed at De Courcy House for a few weeks. Steve was grateful for her presence for it kept Dermot and the gang away from the house. Whenever Sophie disappeared to visit her priest friend, Gloria would announce that she was going upstairs to work on her book. The study windows would open and the smell of incense would drift downstairs.

As soon as Sophie left for London the gang was summoned back and the night-time sessions began again. Steve fought back with evenings at the theatre and invitations to his own friends to join the late-night parties and this helped to control the wildness but the monthly allowance from the trust fund was not enough to support too much entertainment and

Gloria's habit was costing more and more money. She was now well into the pills again and had a network of suppliers. The morning remains of chocolate paper, biscuit wrapping and ice cream cartons informed him of the quantity of sugar needed to "come down" after her sessions of pot smoking and her cry of, "I've got the munchies" was now heard daily as she padded down from the study to raid the larder. He tried detaching himself but she had become secretive about her writing.

There were no requests for help with the typing. He waited until a session with Dermot was in full swing and sneaked into her study to read her latest efforts. Most of it was incoherent rambling about the puppy needing protection from the water and the dachshund taking care of her, then came the new chapter. The dachshund had become cunning, arranging for the puppy to go for long walks with the mongrel while she entertained an exotic poodle from a hotel nearby.

Loneliness engulfed Steve. He wandered to his bedroom to the sound of mad laughter echoing through the corridors. He put the plug into the basin and began to clean his dental plate, aware of the tears dropping into the toothpaste. His chest hurt and he felt tired and insignificant. An old man on the way out. The dogs were draped across the bed. He tried not to disturb them as he plumped his pillows and picked up the Reader's Digest. An hour passed before he realised that even though he had turned the pages he had absorbed nothing but merely gone through the motions while reliving past memories.

He cried himself into a troubled sleep, only to be woken later by cold feet tucked between his knees and the loud rattle of her snores.

*

Sophie returned to London determined to make an effort to understand her mother. In between opening supermarkets for enormous fees, appearing on chat shows and quizzes, she visited Maggie. Vladimir had told her that all revulsion and anger can be cured by love which gives understanding. His quote from St John of the Ladder, "Pride is the extreme poverty of the soul", kept her persevering despite the taunts, insults and malice.

As the weeks passed and Sophie learnt to meet the onslaughts from her mother without becoming emotionally involved, Maggie began to lose some of her resentment and allow Sophie to see the cause of her hatred. She began to confide her fears, her past experiences with men, all disappointing relationships. As the windows were opened and fresh air allowed into the musty house, Sophie discovered that Maggie was starved of love and terrified of feeling anything for anyone. For every chink of vulnerability she would angrily and viciously defend some vile attitude or prejudice.

It was towards the end of October, just before she was due to leave England to start filming, that Sophie experienced the great change. It was after she had been kneeling in front of the icon that Vladimir had given her, chanting the Easter canon of St John Damascene. She had reached "Let us be illumined with the solemn feast. Let us embrace one another, let us say Brethren! and because of the Resurrection forgive all things to those who hate us, and in this wise exclaim: Christ is risen from the dead, trampling down death by death and to all in the grave bestowing life." She had shut her eyes and prayed truly from the heart when the white light grew inside her head and the strength and love filled her entire body. The light was stronger than a thousand suns. It became so bright that she had to open her eyes because it was blinding and frightening. Then there followed the most profound peace. The following day she told Maggie, "Mum, I love you," and she meant it.

Chapter Nine

There was a late morning plane leaving for London. As long as the director kept to the schedule, there was a good chance she could catch it. Sophie had been filming for eighteen weeks, playing the part of a member of the resistance in a war film. She had joined the company in Hungary, travelled with them to West Germany where she had spent Christmas and welcomed in 1971. She had spent the last six weeks on locations in Czechoslovakia. She wasn't needed in Vienna until Monday for dress fittings. With luck, she would be able to meet Steve and Gloria for the birthday tea. Her scene was finished by nine thirty. The director hadn't wasted any time. The idea tickled his sense of humour. "Sophie's rushing back for a fishcake at the Ritz." She was driven to her hotel to change and collect her luggage.

She took a last look at the Alcron and waved to the uniformed commissionaire. The car set off, the tyres rumbling on the cobbles. They circled Wenceslas Square and headed for the airport. She would miss Prague. Her hotel room had been a sanctuary for her thoughts. The skyline of domes and spires had evoked a yearning for an unknown part of herself. On several nights, she had woken to the sound of church bells calling her, only to find when opening the large windows a heavy silence. On her free days she had wandered through the twisting cobbled streets to Charles Bridge, then climbed the winding steps and lanes through Misenska to the

Church of Saint Nicholas. All the time golden symbols and impressive monuments stirred her emotions. At the top of the hill was Saint Vitus and nearby the Golden Lane and Vikarska Street. She had touched the monastery walls and felt that she'd returned from a long journey. She had written down all her thoughts for Vladimir.

The Palm Court was crowded with the rich and famous. Steve listened to the murmured conversation punctuated by the clinking of china and wondered how long Gloria could fool Sophie. When he'd booked the table for March the thirteenth, that had been the signal for her to get into training. She'd become more disciplined, cut down on the drugs and taken the dogs for walks. Sometimes her determination confused him, so that he almost accepted her claim that the addiction was under control. Now he watched her smoking two Gauloises at a time and twiddling with her silver Pisces symbol. She stood up and looked anxiously towards the entrance.

"Sit down Mouse. It's only five after four and she said she'd get here."

"I've got to go to the girl's room."

"Again?"

He watched her totter towards the steps to the Entrance Hall where a waiter helped her down.

The cloakroom attendant watched Gloria's attempt at drawing a smooth line around her lips.

"Are you feeling all right Madam?"

"Yeah, but I have this condition. You're right. Perhaps I ought to take a pill."

"Would you like a glass of water?"

"Thank you dear." Gloria managed to look meek.

Sophie reached the Ritz at four thirty. There was a chorus of happy birthdays and a lot of hugging and kissing. While tea was served and the women gossiped, Steve felt as if he'd had a shot of adrenalin.

They exchanged presents. Sophie gave Gloria a garnet crucifix and Steve some Bohemian goblets. He lifted one of the finely engraved glasses to the light. It brought back the memory of Rosa, the lovely Polish girl whom he had dated just after the war. She had kept some similar glass in her kitchen cupboard. He remembered the tender evening with pleasure. It reminded him of his youth. Sophie was given a bottle of Joy and a Gucci wallet.

Gloria looked at Sophie's thin face. She was a different person from the wild, mad girl she had been a year ago. Gloria worried about her. Sophie had become a vegetarian, got rid of her fur coat and now seemed to be leaning towards religion a bit too much. Gloria had a selection of postcards in Dublin—all sent from different parts of Czechoslovakia —each one with a picture of a church and a message that Sophie had lit a candle for her. Gloria distrusted the Church. To her, the Church was just another finance house selling long-term investment. She would not have left her dogs alone with most of the priests she had met and the nuns who had been in charge of the church-run units where she had dried out had always released her when she shouted "Jesus has saved me" and given a large donation.

People on the adjoining tables looked on curiously when the cake arrived. It was a large goldfish with three candles in the centre. Their names were written in white icing, Sophie by the eye, Gloria over the heart and Steve on the tail. On a count of three, they blew out the candles and wished.

"How long are you going to be in Vienna, Sophie?" Gloria asked.

"Until May, then I have to be in New York for the promotion and opening night of *Daughters of Destiny*."

"Which theatre?" Steve asked.

"Loewe's."

"Gee, I'd love to be there." Gloria looked wistful.

"Why don't you? You could come on to the party . . ."
Sophie watched Gloria's eyes become glazed. She tried putting a Gauloise to her lips but dropped it into her tea. Her
hand lacked the co-ordination needed to lift it out. There was
a moan of frustration and then her body began to shake into a
convulsion. Her mouth dropped open and hung stupidly.

"It's okay Sophie, don't panic. She's okay."

Sophie was shocked by Steve's response. "But Steve, she's
having some sort of fit." He was beckoning a waiter.

"She'll be okay in a couple of minutes."

There was a commotion as Steve and the waiter frog
marched Gloria to the lift. Sophie felt the situation was
unreal. She gathered up their belongings and followed as if in
a nightmare. She felt powerless. The lift took ages to arrive
and when she was dropped at the first floor, she ran along the
corridors desperately listening for the laugh that would mean
that Gloria was safe and well again.

She was propped up on the bed, her eyes staring through
strangely drooping eyelids.

"Are you all right Gloria?" Sophie whispered.

Still staring ahead, Gloria muttered something un-
intelligible and snored.

"Steve, I really think you ought to get a doctor."

"Oh boy, she'd love that."

"But she's almost in a trance. There must be something
seriously wrong with her."

She was shouting and wanting to hit Steve for being so
casual.

"Come on Sophie, wake up. She's an addict for Christ's
sake. She's overdone it this time. If we get a doctor, she'll put
on a big act and he'll prescribe more pills. She knows all the
tricks."

He felt ashamed at losing his temper with her.

"But I thought she'd kicked it Steve. She told me she'd beaten it."

He could hear the same accusing tone that he had once used when ignorantly confronting Gloria's parents and lawyers. Love and loyalty cannot accept the deliberate deceit of the addict. For Sophie's sake, he had to be brutal and force her to see the truth.

"Sophie you're not with her all the time. She sees you for a couple of hours . . ." He stopped her protestations. "No, think about it Sophie, after a couple of hours, she always excuses herself, right?"

Sophie was silent.

"As long as she can fool you, Sophie, she thinks she's got it under control." He saw the tear in the corner of her eye and the wobble of the bottom lip.

"Steve, isn't there something we can do?"

He couldn't bear to see the naive hope that he had once cherished.

"Challenge her Sophie. Tomorrow, let her know that she can't fool you. It's the only way you can force her into any sort of self honesty."

Sophie took a cab from the Arlington Street entrance. She didn't hear the friendly words from the doorman, only the sound of his voice. She was numb and tired. The traffic moved slowly. Saturday night theatre goers mingled with noisy football supporters, heading for a bawdy night in Soho. In the privacy of the taxi, the tears ran down her cheeks. Gloria was part of her strength. She was a partner in recovery. With Gloria's relapse she was aware of her dependence on their friendship and the fear of losing her.

There were clothes to be pressed and packed. Enough for three months. Letters to be sorted. She prowled about the small flat hoping the chores would calm her mind. Perhaps

Vladimir could have helped Gloria. When Sophie had once suggested to Gloria that she might like to meet him, Gloria had refused. With the choice of all or nothing, she had chosen nothing and declared herself an atheist, with no regard for priests. Sophie had not pressed her. She, too, had encountered vicars who were eager to show an actress how worldly they were and obviously had no faith in the way of life they were selling. But Vladimir was different. He was a natural teacher, attracting her respect and attention by the example of his own spiritual life. He demanded nothing, only guided her, sharing with her the fundamental art of living.

On Sunday, they lunched at the Curzon House Club. Steve watched Gloria charm Sophie, tempting her to consider the excuses. She was like a siren luring all around her into her dangerous world of deceit. She explained away her fit as being the result of taking medicine for the 'flu she had caught before leaving Dublin.

"These antibiotics do affect me, you know."

Steve raised his eyes to the heavens. Sophie did challenge her but Gloria insisted that Steve was exaggerating.

"Dear, I occasionally have a little grass to help me relax. The doctor suggested it. He said it wouldn't be harmful to me and he should know."

"Perhaps I should take some pot then." Sophie watched her reaction.

Gloria's eyes narrowed. She rearranged her food on her plate while considering her reply.

"No. Not you. You mustn't touch it. It's different for me."

"Why?"

"Well dear, over the years, my body has built up such an immunity to drugs that it doesn't have the same effect as it would have on you. No, you mustn't touch it."

Sophie knew that Gloria was expressing her love for her

in her own strange way but she persevered with the confrontation.

"But Gloria—all the things you told me, the things you warned me against—you know it's the first pill, the first joint, the first drink. Remember what you taught me. You're lying to yourself Gloria. Why do you hurt yourself? When you do, you hurt us because we love you."

Gloria felt lost. She looked across to Steve and Sophie. All three of them were like fishes, but Steve and Sophie were in the sunlight and she was in the shade and she knew she'd forgotten the way back. Sophie's question had made her ashamed. Like a confused child, she wanted to try. The effort of decision was like lifting a lead weight by the tongue.

"I promise you both I'll try."

"Sure you will," Steve said.

*

Gloria's birthday wish was granted on a sunny day, early in May. They had been playing croquet on the lawns with some visiting friends from Cork. Steve took the call from America. Gloria had just knocked out her opponent when he walked across to deliver the news. She laughed at the thought of her mother dying. The guests interpreted her reaction as one of shock and after offering their sympathies discreetly left. Steve watched her organising the trip. He understood her feelings of triumph. How many times had they talked about what they would do with the vast inheritance. Now the moment had arrived.

Unlike Dublin's lace-like sprawl, New York, from the air, looked like a large pin ball machine. Straight, clean lines of moving cars streamed along like strange fluorescent beads. Gloria had decided to travel alone. She took a last look at the fading, pink sky as the plane began its final descent. The apprehension began inside the airport. After the slow life-style in Dublin, the fast pace of New York came as a shock. It took a while to adjust her ear to the hurried speech and quick decisions. From inside the limousine, she looked up to the towering skyscrapers. This was her city. The place where she was born. They drove through the Mid Town Tunnel to 68th Street and she was deposited at the New York Cornell Hospital. Looking like a suitably distressed daughter, she was led into her mother's room.

The figure on the bed was attached to tubes and wires. The pale eyes focused on her. It was like being a child again and seeing her in her curlers.

"I'll leave you alone with her," the nurse whispered. "Press that bell if there's any change."

"Hello Mother dear."

The eyes glared and there was a gurgle of rage. Gloria made sure that no one could see her then raised her thumbs to her ears and stuck out her tongue. The face on the pillow contorted with fury. More rattling noises hissed from the loose mouth.

"I hope you rot in hell, you bitch."

She watched the writhing and waited for the last gasp before pressing the bell.

The nurse found her crying by the bed.

The car took her straight up First Avenue to 52nd Street. Ten blocks up was Riverside. When she was a child, Greta Garbo would often pass her in the street. Mother always referred to her as Miss Brown. Her mother's apartment looked out on to the East River and Roosevelt Island. Steve had warned her against staying there, so she had booked into the Plaza where she knew Sophie had a suite. The first night of *Daughters of Destiny* was in ten days' time. The chauffeur waited for her. As she approached the entrance to the apartments, she could feel herself regressing. Her feet began to drag and her toes turned inwards.

A coloured maid let her in. Memories swarmed back when she caught sight of the china figurines. They had been moved around on different glass shelves but their smooth, pale faces had the same serene expressions. As a child, she had tried to compete with them. She had made every effort to look like them in the hope of receiving the same loving attention from her mother. Standing awkwardly, in front of the cluster of shepherdesses, was Mother's latest gigolo. Knowing his days were numbered, he had already packed his cases. He showed little surprise or emotion at the news of her death. After a few polite words, he left. Gloria felt no sense of condemnation. Anyone who could put up with Mother deserved every cent he could get.

There was a message left for her at the hotel. Sophie's crowd had gone on to Sardi's and if she felt like joining them, they would be there until ten thirty. She reached the restaurant in time to join them for coffee. The mellow atmosphere and witty gossip restored her equanimity.

"Did you get there in time?" Sophie asked her.

"She died shortly after."

"Sorry."

"Don't be."

An overweight man in an ill-fitting suit with stained lapels sidled up to her.

"I know you, you're Gloria. Remember me, Charlie Gould? I was a friend of Steve's."

"Jesus, Charlie. Of course I remember. How are you? Are you with the film?"

"No, but I handle Bert's personal publicity."

Sophie sighed. Bert was an old star who made small guest appearances in films. He was more famous for his card playing and change of young girlfriends than his acting ability. Directors usually booked him for his entertainment value off the set.

He had worked for two days in Dublin and most of his scene had been cut but he was determined to make as much of his association with the film as possible. Charlie Gould was retained by a few actors like Bert to keep their name in circulation. His main news contacts were cheap gossip writers on down-market journals. Apart from his lewd, boring stories, he was harmless. He hung around the night spots listening for gossip and touting for clients. Gloria seemed to be happy talking with him, so Sophie turned her attention back to the plans for the following day's interview and press calls.

For four days Sophie had been promoted on chat shows, radio phone ins and given "In depth" interviews over breakfast. She had reached the point when her own opinions and pat answers not only bored her but made her feel ashamed. She felt responsible to the one vulnerable teenager who might believe the false, promoted image of herself, or follow the phoney diets or ridiculous beauty treatments. In Glitz City, the legacy from the sixties was an addiction for happiness and the ambition to be a personality. To be listened to or taken notice of, if only for a day. The Big Apple was full of destroyed individuals who, like Icarus, had soared the heights only to have their wings melted by the heat of fame.

Sophie felt each day that her talents were being spent until all that remained was an impoverished soul. At that point she would escape along Fifth Avenue to Saint Patrick's Cathedral to ask forgiveness from her inner self and pray to God the Father for permission to come home. On the other side of Fifth Avenue, a few blocks away, the Rockefeller Centre rose majestically from its sunken plaza. Inscribed in the foundation stone were the words 'Wisdom and Knowledge shall be the Stability of Thy Times'. In New York success was knowledge and euphoria was wisdom. Preachers hustled the air waves for subscribers to truth. Sophie would light a candle in Saint Patrick's and watch the pure natural flame. Remembering Vladimir's words, she would pray from the heart to the Divine Light of all wisdom and knowledge. She would ask for her faith to be strengthened and her anger to be taken away.

"You don't like Charlie, do you?"

"I don't really know him Gloria."

"He's a bit café society but he was very good to Steve and me. You remember I told you I wrote a jewellery column? Well, Charlie got me that. He was around when the big court fight was going on between Mother and me. He'd known Steve in Hollywood. Mother lied through her teeth in the trial but my attorney—Charlie helped Steve to find him—well he totally discredited her during the cross examination. He'd found the Notary Public who'd been in the drug store that night I'd signed the papers. The guy remembered me being drunk. When it was proved that I hadn't known I was signing the deeds giving the rights of my inheritance away or that I was signing in front of a Notary Public because I was so drunk, that was it. I won. I remember Charlie, Steve and I went out for dinner that night."

Sophie was amazed at Gloria's energy. The woman had flown across the Atlantic, experienced her mother's death but was still remarkably bright and talkative. Sophie wondered whether she was on the pills again.

Later, back at the Plaza, in the privacy of Sophie's suite, Gloria became solemn for a while but the knowledge that she was now the heiress to the Van Heerden fortune kept returning her to a strange plateau of exhilaration. She switched her interest to Sophie's imminent big night and the party afterwards, discussing what she would wear and declaring that she had asked Charlie to escort her. Sophie could not catch hold of the old Gloria that she knew. The little woman fluctuated between being an excited child one moment and an authoritative woman the next. Sophie found their relationship had altered. She was now in the role of comforter listening to Gloria's traumatic childhood memories. Then the energy ran out and she became a small, lost mouse. Sophie put her arms around her and Gloria hung on like a child. She broke away, laughing through tears.

"Wouldn't it have been lovely, Sophie, if you had been my mother and I had been yours."

The service was held in the main sanctuary of Saint Bartholomew's Episcopal Church on Park Avenue. Gloria listened to the eulogies. Her mother was described as kind, gracious and beautiful. A generous woman who had given her time and money to countless charities. Representatives of the charities stood reverently in the aisles, praying for the donations to continue. It was only she, it seemed, who had been privy to Mother's darker nature, to have experienced the hate and mental torture that had destroyed her confidence as a child. If it had been possible, her mother would have willed all the money to charity and left Gloria destitute. It was only the Trust, the guardian of the Van Heerden fortune, that had protected her interests.

When her grandfather was discovered in a compromising situation with his male secretary, he had shot himself. That was when her grandmother had drawn up the Trust. The Trust was the law according to Grandma Van Heerden who believed the wrath of God would be passed down for four generations as punishment for her husband's act of sodomy. Whenever she thought of her grandmother, Gloria thought of the colour blue. The old lady wore blue clothes. She had blue curtains and upholstery in her Palm Beach home and when

Gloria stayed with her one Christmas, there was a blue Christmas tree in the lounge. Her other homes in Long Island and in the Mayfair House Hotel had also been decorated throughout in blue. The old lady had loved Gloria and hoped that she might prove to be the good fruit from the sinful Van Heerden family tree.

Gloria's mother had thought she had been smart trapping her father into marriage but she had not been able to out-smart the Trust. After her father died, her mother had convinced the Trustees that Gloria was not mentally fit to control the fund. There was the history of endless hospital treatments to back up her story. So she was given control. But then she became greedy and tried to get a separate legacy in the Trust that Grandmother Van Heerden had set up especially for Gloria. After the court case, in order to protect herself, Gloria had given Steve power of attorney over her money, in case she was ever hospitalised again.

Now she wanted to resume control. Her meeting with the Trustees had gone well. She had been able to explain the feud with her mother and show them that since living in Ireland she had not been treated for any addiction for two years. She now held positions of responsibility with charities and was living a useful, sober life. They had been surprised at her knowledge of money matters and suitably impressed that her marriage had lasted. Two of them attended the service.

Mother was buried in the family plot at Oyster Bay on Long Island. Those attending were impressed by Gloria's composure. The veil hid her smile when the coffin was lowered into the ground. The woman who had taught her the meaning of hell on earth was now being covered by the soil. She tossed the flowers on to the shiny wood in remembrance of the one nanny who had tried to give her some of the love she craved as a child. Mother had sacked her when she knew how fond Gloria was of the woman. She had been six years old. Because she had screamed as she watched the distraught nanny leave, she was locked in the cupboard. That had been the start of her nervous asthma. While the padre uttered words of comfort to the mourners, Gloria cursed her mother to everlasting hell.

*

The limousine glided into Times Square, passing hustlers, tourists and brightly clad teenagers. Sophie sat straight-backed inside, half listening to the nervous comments from her director. The car door opened on to a red carpet and they stepped into a pathway of noisy, shouted instructions, out-stretched hands and exploding flashlights. It was the moment that she dreaded when her heart thudded with fright and her smile became fixed. The conversations swirled through her ears and became alien sounds of gibberish. Among the sea of faces, she spotted her New York agent and his secretary, then they were in the auditorium being escorted to their seats, the people already seated, turning and looking in their direction. She sat between the producer and director. In the row behind, the American publicity chiefs gave orders to their minions, who scurried about the theatre.

The opening credits of *Daughters of Destiny* appeared. Sophie had already seen the film. She closed her eyes and wondered how Gloria was getting on. She had been returning from Long Island just as Sophie was leaving the hotel.

"I'll catch up with you at the Waldorf," Gloria had shouted.

"Are you all right?"

"I'm fine, don't worry about me. Good luck." She had not been slurred or tired looking. On the contrary, she had been very bright and very much in control.

They listened for the audience's reactions. They were

enjoying it. There was a large Irish contingent who cheered loudly at the end.

"It's a hit," the producer said and grabbed her arm. People wanted to touch her, speak with her. Endless compliments were given. She wanted to curl into a ball and roll away but she was transported into the street to the sound of more applause and helped into the limousine.

At the Waldorf, music played and people converging from all directions were introduced. Cameras whirred, microphones hovered. The writer grabbed her hands and gazed into her eyes meaningfully and sincerely. "You look wonderful. You are the heart of the film, Sophie." He eased himself into position for the television cameras and smiled at her adoringly, then spotted an agent he wanted to speak to and moved on. Something deep inside Sophie was rebelling. There was an insane desire to pull off all her finery and scream. She wanted to stand in water and wash away every handshake. To hear silence instead of the gabbling collective madness. Then it happened.

Like a moving stream, the crowd changed its course. T.V. cameras and reporters who had been following her pushed forward in the direction of a tiny, sequined figure who was smoking a Gauloise in a long, jewelled holder. Charlie Gould hovered by her side. Sophie could hear the words: "Van Heerden, heiress, millions." Gloria was being bombarded with questions: "What's it like to be one of the richest women in America? Do you support the IRA? Are you thinking of a career in films?" Sophie watched with fascination as the people swirled around Gloria who was revelling in all the attention. Producers moved closer to her, anxious to be near the money. Professional first-nighters tried to be photographed near her.

There was a loud, braying laugh. "You think I'd make a movie star? Well, how about that?" More delighted shouts of laughter followed. Sophie saw the flushed, excited look on

Gloria's face. She had never seen her so happy. She was star-struck. Thrilled to be thought of as a potential actress. The river of people carried her further away and Sophie was powerless to stop them. Gloria was floating on a high that was impossible to interrupt and Sophie wondered whether she could survive it.

PART THREE

Chapter Ten

Sophie's day began in a preview theatre set in the bowels of Wardour Street.

"See his latest film, Sophie, before you make up your mind about the script. He's the hot director at the moment," Jacob had said. "Then meet me at Rule's."

Sophie emerged later in a mood that matched the weather. She hailed a taxi which ignored her and continued driving towards some Arabs waiting further down the street. Cursing, she ran out into the rain, dodging puddles and weaving in and out of shop doorways en route to Shaftesbury Avenue. The film had been a tasteless cocktail of puberty-stricken sex and slapstick violence. She muttered with rage as she ran. "I think you've got a rotten sense of humour, God. Okay, I need the work but I'm not taking that muck. Or is that what you want me to say? Are you testing me?"

"I should take a bit more water with it darling."

Sophie stopped and grinned at the traffic warden sheltering in the entrance to a strip club.

"I'm taking in plenty of water, ain't I?"

She caught sight of an orange For Hire light as a taxi turned into the street.

"Stop," she screamed, throwing herself across its path.

"Maiden Lane please."

From the safety and warmth of the taxi, she watched the people in Cambridge Circus trying to get out of the rain and wondered whether Jacob had already arrived at the restaurant. She would have to turn the script down, she decided. Jacob would worry and she would feel guilty, especially since he'd been looking very tired during the past few months. The taxi driver began cursing as they became caught up in traffic near the Garrick Club.

"I shouldn't have taken you," he complained, "I was on my way off home, wasn't I?"

He continued to rant, while Sophie bit her nails with irritation and seethed about the weather and the film. She had worked with some of the actors in it and knew them to be good, experienced performers. Sitting in the little preview theatre, watching them squirm and struggle with the puerile dialogue had been embarrassing. But then any director who went on about Meaningful Art, as he had when she'd met him at the Dorchester, had to be suspect. When he had suggested that she should take her clothes off during a car chase and justified his idea as a Meaningful Moment she had wanted to tell him to stuff it. But Jacob's words, "Sophie never be rude—today's schmucks could be tomorrow's important men" were firmly implanted in her brain.

"You're soaked through, my darling." Jacob looked soft, clean and gentle against a background of plush wallpaper.

"You've got to be an Arab to get a taxi these days."

"My darling, they're everywhere." He sympathised. "I hear they're even giving cars as tips, they have so much money to throw about. So." He leant back and looked at her expectantly. "What did you think of the film?"

"The only thing hot about that director, Jacob, is the hot air in his publicity blurb."

"Another dirty film?"

"Drivel."

"I don't want you doing such films Sophie. Perhaps I ought

to try and get you into T.V. A lot of people are doing it these days—there are so few films about."

"It's all right Jacob, I can wait."

He ordered the steak and kidney pudding, insisting as usual that she should eat more because she needed to put on weight and then gossiped wickedly about various actors' love lives. He reserved the serious news until after they had eaten the elaborate sweet.

"I want you to be the first to know, Sophie. I want to retire in September."

"Oh."

"Bob Cantor's going to take over. You met him at one of our get-togethers. You'll like him. Very shrewd boy. A hustler. I'm getting too old Sophie. The clients need a younger man. All the producers I knew have either died or become the past. Secretaries are now the casting directors. I can't remember their names. Bob knows all these secretaries."

"It won't be the same without you, Jacob."

"I'm not dying, just retiring. I'll be keeping an eye on you, my Sophie. Henry and I have found a lovely flat on the front in Hove. You could come down at weekends, the fresh air would do you good."

"Is there room for me to stay sometimes?"

His face lit up and his hands gesticulated like a geisha. "We've a room we're calling Sophie's room. You can stay any time you like. Henry's already got our name down for a beach hut." He giggled. "Can you see us dear, sitting in our deck-chairs with all the Jewish ladies? My mother always wanted to live in Hove, God bless her."

Sophie listened to him extol the virtues of Hove and enthusiastically describe his plans for furnishing. She felt an enormous sense of relief. With Jacob's imminent retirement, she felt less guilty for her waning ambition.

For the past six months, she had become increasingly

aware that she was going through the motions of enjoying her career, purely to justify Jacob's faith in her. All the sense of urgency to win parts in films had been replaced by a restless yearning. At first she had wondered whether it was the need for a mate but after dating several interesting men, she knew that it was not the desire for a man that was causing such longing. While she watched Jacob's mouth listing his friends in Brighton, she pondered on what life would be like if she gave up guilt.

They shared a taxi as far as the Ritz.

"You're very special to me Sophie," Jacob said.

"And you are to me. I owe everything to you."

"You know when I tell the other clients about my retiring, I know none of them will think about what's best for me. They'll all moan about themselves. Not like you, my little love. Shalom, my Sophie."

When he kissed her head, she could smell the sweet scent of lavender on his skin.

"Mr and Mrs O'Connell are in their suite, Miss Smith. Shall I ring through to them for you?"

"Yes please."

The desk clerk smiled as he dialled. "I loved your last film, if you don't mind me saying so. My wife didn't but I did. Oh, here you are now. I have Miss Smith in the foyer, Mrs O'Connell."

Sophie took the receiver eagerly. "I'm here," she announced happily and waited for a zany response.

Gloria's voice croaked back, "Sophie, you're early. I'm just changing. Do you want to come up?" She sounded slightly put out.

"Well," Sophie hesitated, disappointed at the lack of delicious madness. "No, it's all right. I'll wait down here, at the table." She wandered towards the Palm Court and looked for Michael. At first she thought that she was the only one there until she spotted a middle-aged man, dressed in tweeds, eating sandwiches behind a large German newspaper. Michael announced himself by a discreet cough and showed her to a place in the corner.

"Wait until you see the birthday cake, Miss Smith. The chef really enjoyed making it." He spoke with her until another group of people arrived when he left her to usher them across the room.

Sophie watched one of the women, who was dressed in high fashion, mince towards the table. She was balanced precariously on high platform shoes. Sophie's back ached in sympathy. The woman lowered herself uncertainly into a chair and turned a heavily made-up face in her direction. Sophie wriggled her toes in her comfortable boots and wondered why a lot of women wanted to look like female transvestites. Gloria often nagged her about not being more interested in fashion but could not understand when Sophie explained that she wanted to be a person and not a mincing parody of a woman.

More arrivals were taking their seats. Sophie laid out her presents and patiently waited for the two Americans.

Waiters hovered. The hum of conversation grew louder over the sounds of rattling china and clinking cutlery. Sophie thought of Jacob and his impending retirement. She wanted to change her life but was unsure of the path to take. The past three months had been like a dark night of the soul, with every attempt at self promotion an assault on her inner self. There had been a fight on between her mind and her emotions. When she had read some of the scripts sent to her, there had been an overwhelming sense of destructive negativity. As if some living continuity of life was slipping away. She had written to Vladimir telling him about the need within which she could not explain or share and he had replied with sympathetic understanding. "I, too, have been through that inner turmoil, Sophie. It is hard to explain a desire that is beyond intellectual or psychological analysis. You will find comfort from reading the gospels. They have been inspired by the Divine Light of love and when received with an open heart, give mental illumination. I pray for you daily, dear Sophie . . ."

It startled her when Steve touched her arm. Whenever she thought of Vladimir, time ceased to exist.

"Gloria's decided to change again. How are you?" He hugged her. She noticed that his complexion was tinged with a slight blue colour and he appeared very tired. "She's bought up London," he went on. "I can't tell you how many art fart fund-raising dinners we've been to since we arrived."

"Don't tell me you didn't enjoy them Steve." She started to laugh. He was continually moaning about Gloria's wish to be the great patron of the arts. It meant escorting her around various art galleries when all he wanted to do was some quiet fishing or to be reading a book.

"Sophie, we've got all these paintings we're taking back to Dublin. Weird things, some of them. Gloria pretends she knows what they're about. Did I tell you that Dermot wanted to paint one of our walls. Luckily, it's not allowed in the lease." Sophie chuckled at the idea of Celtic whorls plastered over the walls of De Courcy House. "It's good to see you Sophie," he went on, "I was having a nap when you phoned. That is, as much of a rest as one can have with Gloria around. You know, yesterday I met up with the boys at El Vino's for lunch while she was having another hair-do. It was good to see them again too. And they asked me what it was like to be married to Gloria. And I said, 'Well, I guess I got used to it.' What do you think of that?" He paused, remembering the occasion. "Well," he smiled ruefully, "I suppose *Tender is the*

Night could be summed up by a paragraph in Hickey." He examined his cufflinks in silence.

"How bad is it?"

"She's on uppers today. You know how it is—one day up then one day down. Did you know we had a bomb scare here earlier?"

"No."

"Sure was a lot of activity. One of your politicians was here and they hurried him out. Yesterday, the boys were asking me what I thought about the IRA movements in Dublin. I told them that the Maoists had infiltrated the Provos. You know your writers in Wicklow didn't know about it when I told them. They're too busy quarrelling about who had their picture in the Sunday supplements. You know the sort of thing—tax exiles in Ireland and all that."

"Happy birthday Sophie," Gloria shouted the greeting across the room and proceeded to stagger across the carpet on very high-heeled suede boots, the colour of which matched her suede maxi suit. Under her arm, she carried a beautifully wrapped present and Sophie was pleased to see the glint of the little silver fish at her throat.

"Sophie, did you know George Washington was a Pisces?"

"No."

"Neither did I. It was in your *Times* today." She crashed down into the chair and while the tea was being served talked about all the functions she and Steve had attended since arriving in London. Steve tried to join in the conversation but Gloria continued talking across everything he said. "Did Steve tell you there was a bomb scare in the neighbourhood?"

"They should have blown up that art gallery we went to yesterday. It would have done everyone a favour." Steve smiled with triumph.

"He just has no art appreciation dear. It was very fine, modern art—a friend of Dermot's."

"I suppose that makes it good. Me, I just like to see what I'm supposed to be seeing."

Sophie listened to them bickering. Gloria had developed a twitch on the left side of her face since she had last seen her. She interrupted them by presenting her slightly crumpled parcels. "Happy birthday you two fish," she said.

"And you too darling," said Gloria.

Sophie had bought Steve a book of fishing tales and found some fish shaped ashtrays for Gloria to use in the bedroom. The last time that she had visited De Courcy House, she had noticed that Gloria's sheets looked as if they had been sprayed by a machine gun. Close inspection of the holes showed that they were the result of many dropped cigarette ends. Gloria gave her an evening bag.

The cake was a silver blue whale. Inside the moist sponge was lemon butter filling. Gloria actually stopped talking to blow out the candles and then she was off again. Steve looked at Sophie and shrugged his shoulders. Gloria was repeating the stories that she had told them a few minutes earlier. Sophie felt that she was listening to a stranger. She wanted to reach for her hand and pull her out of this rambling current of fatuity.

"How's the book coming along Gloria?"

"Well dear, I really haven't had the time what with one thing and another . . ."

"Sophie please," Steve interrupted, "last year it was literature, this year it's art." He coughed and loosened his collar. The cake was sitting in his throat and the Gauloises and Gloria's voice had given him a headache. He excused himself and wandered off towards the Piccadilly entrance for some air.

Sophie stared into the large black expressionless pupils. Gloria was on speed. No wonder she couldn't stop talking. "You're back on the pills aren't you?" she said.

Gloria's eyes did not even flicker but focused on a point in the middle of Sophie's forehead. "No dear, I'm just taking my hormone pills and some vitamin E." She started to retell another story and Sophie felt lost. There was no honesty left. Only a series of automatic reactions, rehearsed conversations and nervous gestures. The warm human personality had disappeared.

"It was a lovely cake," Sophie whispered.

The pale afternoon sunshine had brought some colour to Piccadilly. Steve watched the people queuing for buses, hailing taxis or crossing Green Park on their way to Victoria station. It never ceased to amaze him that he only had to take a few steps away from Gloria to be in a normal world again. He breathed in deeply, trying to fill the furthest pocket of lung, so that it might rid him of the taste and smell of Gauloises. He followed the commuters into the park, wistfully listening to their everyday conversations. Bold daffodils swayed in the slight breeze. The sight of their spring gaiety brought tears to his eyes which he angrily brushed away. He heard the sound of a girl's laugh which reminded him of Sophie's smile when she opened her present. Gloria had put a cheaper bag into a box from one of her own expensive purchases, then got the housekeeper to wrap it up for her. The girl had not noticed. She had been happy with the present but Steve had felt ashamed. Why was Gloria so mean with those who loved her when she would throw money at creeps like Dermot? She would write a large cheque for a charity and then quibble over a small increase in Maureen's wages. She had opened an account for him for a quarter of a million dollars and then hollered blue murder when she found out he'd sent some to his ex-wife.

He watched some ducks clamber out of the water and shake their feathers. Was Gloria becoming bored with

Sophie, he wondered. All the signs of irritation were there. She was continually criticising the way the girl dressed or complaining that she did not make the most of herself. The truth was that Sophie did not behave the way that Gloria thought a successful actress should, so she had tried to manipulate Sophie in the same way that Gloria's mother had tried to do with her. Steve surprised himself with the discovery. That was something he would save as a bombshell when she pushed him too hard, he decided. He could hear himself saying it to her, "You have become just like your goddam mother." He wandered back to the hotel in time to catch Sophie as she left.

"She's gone up to change for the charity ball, Steve."

"Well, that'll take hours. And besides, all she needs is a cheque book."

"Steve, what are we going to do? She's got really bad now."

"Sophie, do you really want to know what you can do for Gloria?"

"Of course I do."

"Well dear, try to remember her as she was when you first met her. Because that was Gloria at her best."

"Don't say that Steve. You're talking as if she were dead."

"A part of her is dead," he said sadly. "I guess that part died with her mother."

When Sophie reached her flat she found a message from Jacob on the answering machine.

"Sophie dear, I've just had an offer for you from Walt Disney. It sounds a nice film for you. Eight weeks in France from the second week in May. They're sending you the script. Read it and let me know what you think. And start eating a few more meals, my little love."

She unwrapped the remains of the blue whale cake and lit the three candles again. "Remember Gloria as she was,"

Steve had said. Sophie pined for the old Gloria. For the loving friend whose soul had slipped into some lost land. "Please God," she whispered, "let me help her to come back. But I don't know what to do." She wondered whether they had just had the last birthday celebration at the Ritz and the tears streamed down her cheeks.

Taking a candle that Vladimir had given her, she lit it and placed it in front of her icon. She watched as the lights from the three candles on the cake gradually spluttered out, while the flame from the tall, amber candle continued to illuminate the room.

*

Easter Saturday fell on April the first and the O'Connells threw an Easter Bunny and April Fool party. De Courcy House was thronged with jesters and rabbits of all shapes and sizes. A band played from inside a large cardboard Easter egg in the ballroom and extra staff had been brought in to help with the catering. It was dawn before the last revellers departed, leaving a tired jester to carry a bunny with bent ears up the stairs to bed.

There were rabbits and jesters in Gloria's dream. They carried her laughing and shouting all the way back to Camp Happy where the girls were waiting for her. They all cheered and clapped her when the jesters presented them with presents but then everyone turned and ran away, leaving her alone again. She wanted to find Meg. A gust of wind blew her to the river bank where she could see her friend swimming in the water. She was laughing and leaping out of the river like a silver-blue fish.

"Come on in."

"But I can't swim."

"Yes you can."

Gloria lowered her feet into the water and the soothing

167

warmth crept up around her thighs. Then she was swimming easily into the deeper water where she could see the back of Meg's head. The blonde hair began to move away from her and the cold currents swirled through her legs. Icy tentacles of frozen weed wrapped themselves round her waist.

"Meg," she cried.

The head in front of her turned and she found herself looking into the dead eyes of her mother.

She woke up screaming and thrashing the bed only to feel the wetness of the sheet. Mortified, she felt between her legs but found she was dry. The large, soaking patch was coming from Steve's side of the bed. She shook his shoulder but there was no response.

"Goddammit Steve." She fumbled with the light and managed to crawl out of bed, her head reeling from the effects of Mandrax.

"You've gone and wet the bed, goddammit," she shouted from the floor while she clumsily pulled at the bedclothes.

"Steve, wake up."

There was no reply.

"Stop fooling Steve." She scrambled up to him and shook his shoulder roughly. Then she felt the coldness of his skin. She could not cry or make any sound. She sat on his chest and tried to shake the life back into him. Maureen found her later, whimpering and pulling at his hair.

*

As Sophie approached the Russian Orthodox church on Saturday night, she could hear the bells heralding Easter. She followed the procession towards the great screen of icons and stood among the sea of faces, each one lit by an individual candle's flame. The resonant singing and chanting of the canon evoked strange, mysterious memories from a time before. An inner echo responded to the unaccompanied priest's salute. She thought of the salt in tears and seas, sulphur in war and earth, and her soul cried to return to where she belonged. Her family, work and present life were but passing moments on a brief journey.

"Lord, I have cried unto thee, hear me. Hear me, O Lord . . . Bring my soul out of prison, that I may confess thy name."

She found new meaning in the word "mother". She whispered it and let the loving embrace of mother church envelop her. The perfume of incense, the vibration of voices, the banners and icons, welcomed her home. "Christ is risen from the dead, trampling down death by death and bestowing life to those in the tomb."

The seed had fallen on fertile ground that Vladimir had seen, tended and nourished until the season arrived. Sophie walked back to Nell Gwynn House on Easter Sunday, new in spirit and with a profound peace in her heart. When she slept, she dreamed of forests and hills, saw caves with makeshift altars and walked by a white sea to the sound of the bells she'd heard calling her in Prague.

She slept until midday and then caught a train to Hove where she stayed with Jacob and Henry for a few days. They were proud of their flat and took a delight in showing her the pink "Sophie" room with the bathroom en suite. The weather was warm enough for them to take deckchairs and a picnic on to the beach, where she paddled while they slept. They fed her until she was at bursting point and escorted her like two excited nannies along the Palace Pier, making sure they tried everything including a bone rattling ride on the ghost train. Pink-faced and relaxed she returned on Wednesday night to London.

She had only been in the flat for twenty minutes when Maureen telephoned with the news of Steve's sudden death.

She arrived in Dublin the following evening, desperately

hanging on to the memory of their last meeting at the Ritz and Steve's words of advice: "Remember Gloria as she was." But when she was confronted by the manic personality, babbling inanities, who dragged her into the lounge to introduce her to a group of stupid, vacuous potheads, it was almost impossible to think of Gloria as anything but a deranged monster.

There were about twenty people sprawled around the room, smoking grass and listening to John Lennon's music. Even the dogs looked stoned. One of them had deposited a turd which rested obscenely by a pile of magazines. "We're giving Steve a wake," a giggling young man announced and proceeded to spout some banal poetry. Sticks of incense smouldered, releasing a sickly, sweet smell into the tawdry atmosphere. Sophie felt she had stepped into an insane hell of tongues flicking over cigarette papers and mouths that rambled out sermons of such triviality that to Sophie it seemed a blasphemy of life itself.

"I expect you'd like to go to your room, Sophie."

Maureen was a welcome sight of normality, albeit a nervous one.

"Sophie what are we going to do?" she whispered as they climbed the stairs. "She's off her head. If she's not out cold on the bed, she's in this state with them."

Sophie tried to remain calm. Gloria shouted from the hall.

"I'm just going to unpack Gloria, won't be long."

"I'll come up and help."

"Would you like me to bring you a cup of tea later, Sophie?" Maureen said, "And we can talk."

"All right."

Gloria tottered into the bedroom scattering ash every-where as she entered. In the brightness of the bedroom light, Sophie could see her glazed eyes staring out from dark, purple hollows. She talked non stop about how she had found Steve and then about how Dermot had promised to paint his portrait from an old photograph. Sophie watched her re-enact the drama, performing the macabre ritual around the bed. She put her arms around her and Gloria became still for a moment before beginning the story again, using the same words and repeating the motions. Sophie unpacked her case, concentrating on the clothes in an attempt to control her emotions. Gloria's voice, the sounds of music and odd high pitched giggles drifting up from the lounge, were beginning to affect her. Her throat felt full and she knew she was verging on the edge of panic. The thought of having a vodka flashed through her mind. Gloria finished her cigarette and searched the air, confused by the absence of an oral prop. She lost interest in what she was saying and wandered back down-stairs.

Sophie opened the windows and breathed in deeply. The fact that she had momentarily thought of a drink frightened her. She listened to the waves pulling through the shingle and remembered the first meeting with Steve and Gloria two years ago, when they had the first birthday cake. The sea continued to caress the shore while her harsh sobs racked the soft night air. Maureen crept in and discreetly rattled the cup and saucer. It was bright orange, sweet tea. Sophie gulped it down and prayed silently while Maureen talked.

"It's been terrible. It was bad enough before Steve died but now, it's awful. And how is she going to cope with the funeral tomorrow? You can't wake her in the mornings."

The hot drink and concentration on prayer had revived some of Sophie's strength.

"Let me think Maureen. Let me think what Steve would have done."

"Nothing, that's the trouble. That bloody Dermot thinks he owns the place. Wanders about . . ." Maureen listed Dermot's exploits and Sophie became angry.

"Why don't we report him to the drug squad?"

"We can't Sophie. Mrs O'Connell might get involved and Steve said she would lose her Trust or something."

"That damned Trust." Sophie groaned. "If I were a man, Maureen, I'd throw him out."

"Sophie listen. I've got a cousin. You promise not to tell anyone mind."

"What?"

"You promise?"

"I promise."

"Well, he's with the IRA. I could get him to take care of him."

"Not to kill him?"

"He could warn him off."

"But they mustn't kill him Maureen."

"No, they could just threaten him a bit."

"Oh, I'm not sure. Let me think about it."

Dermot and his cronies were raiding the refrigerator. Sophie went in search of Gloria and found her in the lounge, lying unconscious on the sofa. The dogs were beside her, their paws held limply in the air. She returned to the kitchen to confront Dermot. Aware that Maureen was watching, she tried to sound in command of the situation.

"What's Gloria taken, Dermot?"

The bearded man chewed happily at some bread and jam. There was no aggressive reaction from him. He smiled, indifferent to her challenging tone and casually replied, "Tuis, I think. Perhaps some blues too. Sad lady, Gloria."

He inspected the bread with reverence. Sophie could not sustain her anger. Dermot and his friends were in a world of soft dreaming. They ignored her and talked and laughed together in a strange, incoherent jargon of their own. She looked across at Maureen who was going through the pretence of clearing up. The woman's back was bristling with rage. But these people were not really exploiting Gloria, Sophie thought. They were inadequate, childish people whose attitude towards Gloria was that as she possessed money and comfort, they had a right to share it with her. Gloria had not been corrupted by them. She had willingly, knowing full well the dangers, bought herself into the sickness. Only she was responsible for her own addiction. Sophie thought of Steve's enduring patience and his rueful sense of humour and realised how much he must have loved the sick woman.

"Dermot."

He turned a drugged face towards her and focused his eyes slowly.

"We have to get Gloria ready for Steve's funeral. Would you mind taking all your friends home now?" She felt like a warped Mary Poppins.

"Sure Sophie, no sweat."

It was another hour before they left, leaving a trail of debris behind them. With Gloria safely in bed, Maureen and Sophie were able to plan their campaign against her addiction. Their first task was to find her hoard of drugs. The search lasted until one in the morning and revealed quantities of pills, hash and cocaine hidden in unlikely places such as the butter compartment in the refrigerator, eggboxes, shoeboxes, and they found the marijuana inside an old pair of tights, stuffed up the chimney in the study. The two women gathered it all up and ceremoniously dumped it into the large outside drain. As they watched thousands of pounds-worth disappearing, their whispering gave way to a hysterical laughing. They collapsed exhausted in the dining room.

"Oh Sophie, I haven't looked so hard since I used to play hunt the thimble with my granny."

"Can you imagine the state of the rats in the sewers?"

Sophie was weak with laughter. "They'll be bombed out of their minds for months."

In the morning the hilarity was forgotten as they tried to wake Gloria. Neither shouting nor slapping could rouse her. Finally they dunked her into a bath which brought about a series of whimpering protests until her confused brain accepted that they were trying to prepare her for the funeral. They dressed her as if she were a helpless child, easing each limp finger into her black gloves, then they propped her up on a chair until Michael arrived to carry her down to the car.

The journey to Dublin was a nightmare. It was as if Gloria was torn between extreme remorse for the state she was in and the wish to remain in oblivion. She kept lighting cigarettes and then promptly dropped them into her lap. She called Sophie Meg, and then cried her apologies to Steve. Sophie bit her lip until it was bruised. She could hear Maureen's muffled sobs and knew she had to be strong enough to pull them all through the service.

The Mercedes circled Saint Stephen's Green and turned into Dawson Street. While Maureen adjusted the black veil over Gloria's dazed face, Sophie spoke firmly to her right ear. "Now, we're getting out of the car."

Michael helped them to carry her into Saint Ann's porch where they each took an arm.

"Are you ready Maureen?"

"Ready."

The church was packed with people. Steve had had many friends and they had come to pay their respects. Also dotted among the box-like pews were some local bigwigs from Gloria's charities. Sophie was aware of the curious glances as they frog marched her along what seemed to be a mile long aisle.

"Sit," Sophie whispered and Gloria's limp body folded into the wooden seat, dropping her bag on to the floor. While

Sophie held her upright, Maureen gathered up all the paraphernalia, trying to make as little noise as possible.

They hoisted her up for the hymns and pulled her down for the prayers. Sophie stared ahead at the altar and concentrated her attention on the meek lamb in the centre of the golden mosaic reredos. The dignified vicar glided across to the pulpit and paused while he wiped his spectacles. Sophie looked up at the stained-glass windows above the gallery and the mural tablets erected in memory of devout citizens from another time and prayed that it would not be too long before the organ could drown the snuffles and groans coming from Gloria's hunched up body. During the sermon, she either snored or farted. As the service ended, she announced that she hated her mother.

As Sophie and Maureen propelled her out of the church, Gloria's feet skimmed over the parquet flooring. Sophie was grateful there was to be no burial service. Steve's body was being sent to Northern Ireland for cremation. The ashes would be returned to Black Rod cemetery later.

"Put your right hand out and say 'Thank you vicar'," Sophie said.

Gloria was like a rag doll. First her knees would buckle and then her head would roll forward. She waved a distracted hand towards the concerned vicar and slurred the words. Michael helped them to carry her to the car but once she was safely inside, she became restless, fidgeting with her face and hair then pulling at her dress.

"Michael, take me to the chemist," she demanded.

Sophie took a deep breath and prepared herself for battle. "No," she said, "we're not going to the chemist. Straight home Michael."

"But I have to have my prescription." Gloria wailed. The cursing and yelling that followed was the overture to a grand madness. Michael drove the Mercedes like a getaway car while the three women dressed in black shouted at each other behind him.

By the time Doctor Hennessy arrived, Sophie was beginning to panic. The dogs were barking and the house was in uproar as Gloria crashed about looking for the missing drugs. When Sophie explained how she had thrown everything out, the doctor was furious with her and straightaway rushed up the stairs, followed quickly by a nurse. Later, when she told him how Steve and Gloria had helped her to come off the drink, he was more sympathetic.

"I know you meant well, Sophie, but you must understand that Gloria's case is quite different from yours. Her chemical tolerance is much higher. For her to come off everything at once is extremely dangerous." He approved of her dumping the cocaine and marijuana. "But she needs careful detoxification for the pill withdrawals." He stayed for a while sipping tea and talking to her about *Daughters of Destiny* and complimenting her on her performance. "But you've lost a lot of weight since you made that film. Do you suffer from anaemia?"

"I don't think so."

"Well, I'll bring some iron pills with me when I come tomorrow."

The nurse would return shortly and stay for a week, he told her. She would deal with Gloria and administer any pills that she needed.

"Now I warn you. In a few days she'll be more lucid. That's when you must take great care that she doesn't manipulate you into getting her more pills."

Sophie promised him that she would stay on her guard.

She sat by the side of the bed listening to the snorting, choking sounds as Gloria slept. Gently, she turned her on her side and brushed away the strands of hair smeared across her mouth. Steve had been right to call her Mouse, Sophie thought. Her thin little arms and bony shoulders had the same translucent sheen as a newly born white mouse. She tucked the coverlet around her before going back downstairs. Maureen had opened all the windows and doors. Sophie could hear her in the kitchen preparing supper. The lounge was cleared of all the chaos and instead of the rancid smell of Gauloises, the perfume from a vase of lilac filled the room. The nurse sat by the window, quietly knitting a baby jacket. She looked up as Sophie crossed the room.

"Was Mrs O'Connell still sleeping?"

"Yes. I turned her on to her side."

"She'll be fine for a couple of hours." She continued knitting at an incredible speed.

Close by the french windows, the dogs were basking in the late afternoon sunshine. When they saw Sophie cross the lawn, they stirred themselves and waited expectantly. She walked slowly and thoughtfully, her hands thrust deep into the pockets of her jeans. She felt ashamed for the lack of knowledge about Gloria's complicated addiction and for the fact that she had considered herself a friend and yet been so unaware of Steve's lonely problems. She realised with sadness that she had never loved anyone as much as Steve had loved Gloria. Her own brief courtship and even briefer marriage had never been built on real love but on romantic illusion. Her pride had been hurt more than her heart when it had ended.

She wandered down to the beach where the dogs caught up with her barking excitedly. She remembered her first lessons in kindness and love from Jacob and Henry, then the example of loyal love given by Gloria and Steve. She thought of Vladimir and how he had removed the icy splinter from her heart with spiritual love. The sun was turning the sky into a dome of rose red veins as it sank into the sea. She stood and watched the red orb. "I'm thirty-two," she said to the fading light, "and I'm only just beginning to learn how to love."

She watched the sea reflecting the colour of the sunset and prayed for the strength and endurance she would need to help Gloria.

Gloria was in another world where her mouth and brain were unable to co-ordinate and give voice to her confused thoughts. Her body was numb which was a relief from the prickling and tingling but she wanted to feel some sensation in her feet or legs and her mind couldn't concentrate. Sophie sounded as if she was talking through a tank of water. Gloria started to cry. Why had Sophie done this to her? She watched the girl come closer and take her hand. She and Steve were keeping her a prisoner so that they could have an affair. She spat out the accusation and dug her nails into the girl's arm. Her mother, dressed in white, was covering her hands. Her spine chilled as she was turned and smothered into the blackness of a cupboard.

Nurse Kelly shepherded Sophie to the door.

"No. Now you're to take a break. She'll be as nasty as this for quite a few days more."

Sophie was shaking with emotion. The swing from Gloria's little girl lost act to the one of foul screaming abuse, was frightening. The black hideous fantasies that crawled out of Gloria's subconscious were like the contents of Pandora's box released into the world to plague her. She had spent much time sifting through her own dark areas of thought and hoped she'd confronted them all. But listening to Gloria made her wonder what other evils lurked within her own self, waiting for the opportunity to escape.

Grey clouds were gathering over Dublin as Michael dropped her off at Wellington Road on his way into the city. She walked quickly towards the sanctuary of Vladimir's cottage. The air in the small lane was heavy with the scent of wallflowers that grew out of the cracks in the old stone walls. The old priest greeted her warmly and led her into the quiet lounge. The glow from the hearth and pungent smell of peat restored her sense of security. She relaxed into her favourite armchair and listened to the gentle clink of the cups as he arranged the familiar tea things. She felt content just to be near his quiet presence. He brought in a plate of chocolate biscuits.

"And how is your friend now, Sophie?"

She told him about the changes of mood and the dark, horrific imaginings that had been part of Gloria's withdrawals.

"I'm frightened that there's just as much evil and filth inside me—and I wonder what it would take to bring it all out."

"Come with me and let me show you something," said Vladimir. He led her through a small walled garden to a little goldfish pond. "Do you see that strange, half cocoon-like thing clinging to that reed?"

"Yes."

"Well, once it was an ugly creeping creature in the sludge and slime at the bottom of the pond. Then at a certain time, it knew it had to change its form. It became a pupa, still beneath the water but detached from its familiar world of mud. Now it answers a call that offers a new life. It slowly and painfully climbs this reed, knowing it now belongs to a world of light and air. It is hard and difficult, for it is half a new being and yet half remains inside the pupa. Soon it will emerge as a dragonfly. This transformed creature will add beauty and colour to the world. And it will serve an important purpose. It will destroy the mosquitoes that suck the blood from man."

Rain was beginning to fall. Sophie watched the large drops gather momentum so that the pond became a series of expanding and colliding circles. They hurried back to the fireside where Vladimir continued his analogies between the metamorphosis in nature and the spiritual development within the individual. She shared with him her own tentative spiritual awakening and he told her about his early manhood and the battles with his mind and thoughts.

"You know Sophie, I too had a friend. As close I think as your friendship with Gloria. Alexei. Ah," he sighed, "there was someone who was born pure. Who never knew the conflict and inner turmoil that I experienced. But he would help me with the same stories I am telling you."

"Where is he now?"

"He died. Well . . ." Vladimir paused and stared into the fire. Sophie watched the crinkles by his eyes which she always remembered as formed by humour, droop with pain. He stirred his tea for a while and then continued softly. "It was during the purge . . . He was in the Solovetzk monastery . . . It is on an island in the White Sea . . . It became a prison and a lot of terrible things happened there . . . He was shot trying to escape . . . He died in the sea."

Sophie watched the smoke rise from the peat and silently sympathised with her friend's sorrow. "To lose a member of your family is always painful, Sophie, but to lose a friend, someone who shared your secret thoughts, inspired you with loyalty and with whom you laughed over the ridiculous until tears came . . . Well, it is a great loss in one's life." He got up from the chair and went to a little box on the mantelpiece.

"He was a very gifted silversmith. Even as a boy he liked to make things. He made me this." He handed her a small silver fish. "And gave it to me when I too became a priest."

Sophie felt a strange warmth in her spine and looked down at the finely worked piece resting in the palm of her hand. She closed her fingers around it and just for a moment she saw spires and heard the faint sound of bells. Reluctantly, she handed it back to Vladimir.

"It's beautiful."

He nursed the fish and looked at her thoughtfully.

"You know Sophie, at the moment we live in a world where men are drowning in the dark waters of political confusion. Materialism has replaced many of the higher ideals and a battle is being fought for our minds and souls."

He put the little fish back into the box on the mantelpiece and continued to address the fireplace as if he were hearing the thoughts before passing them on to her.

"With the traditions of our mother church, which we feel from within, we climb that slender reed and hold on to our faith. We witness the spirit's revelations and we grow into children of God." He turned to look at her carefully, stroking his beard. Seeing he still had her attention he went on, "And then begins the war. We fight the ignorance and apathy that would drain men of their spiritual life's blood. Oh Sophie, the disciples of the new age must be spiritual warriors. Their faith and prayers must be rods of light to guide the yet unborn of the next generation." He smiled at the earnest expression on her face. "While you are here this time, you must see the other Ireland Sophie. Not the Ireland of your friend's world but the country which I consider to be my spiritual home."

A few days later, he arrived at De Courcy House in a battered Ford Escort. Balanced precariously on the back seat was a basket in which he had packed a picnic.

"I am taking you through Enniskerry and on to Glendalough Sophie. The Glen of two lakes. It is also known as the city of seven churches and is one of the most special places I know. So beautiful and so peaceful."

After passing through Bray, they turned off on to smaller roads that led up to rolling hills. Into the car drifted the scents of grasses and blossom with the occasional warm, rich smell from farms. Vladimir drove slowly, unperturbed by the odd car that worried his back bumper aggressively waiting to pass.

"Do you want to listen or talk or just be?" he asked, concentrating on the curving, twisting road.

She felt no need for speech. The silences between them were an expression of trust. She felt awe and a sense of wonder at the sight of the majestic countryside. Vladimir pointed out the odd pieces of rag tied by the wayside that were tinkers' signals for other gypsies that there was a camp not far away. They drove past it further along. Children and dogs chased about between old cars, women hanging washing over branches and men who were fixing engines, sitting on caravan steps smoking or chopping wood.

They meandered along narrow lanes between high grasses and picnicked high in the hills where they watched the changing light on the face of Sugar Loaf mountain. Down below, sprinkled across the valley, were wild flowers, gorses, shrubs and the small figures of grazing sheep.

While they ate, Vladimir told her about the times when saints arrived in Ireland to set up monasteries and places of learning. Like Saint Kiaran who founded Clonmacnois right in the heart of the country, on the banks of the Shannon. And when Dublin was called Baile Atha Cliath. While he talked, she watched the shadows from the clouds dappling the hills, changing the green of the grass. This Ireland would outlive all materialism, she thought. She could feel the country's spirit. The world of vegetation sang its hymn and filled the air with joy. They arrived at the Glendalough monastic site late in the afternoon.

"This was built by Saint Kevin in the sixth century," Vladimir informed her.

The crumbling stone monastery with its tall tower and ancient tombstones sprawled down towards a small bridge under which a clear stream chuckled its way across moss-covered rocks. While Vladimir wandered silently among the ruins absorbing the tranquillity and spirituality of the place, Sophie stood on the bridge and watched the water flowing down towards the lake. During every moment of its journey it reflected light. She looked towards Vladimir who was standing quite still and gazing in the direction of some bay trees. Near him was an old Celtic cross. She moved across to look at the ancient stone monument. Behind it was a background of dark, green yews and rising against the skyline the hills cast their mysterious shadows across the glen. She looked up to the sky. Every molecule appeared to be dancing with its own light, like myriads of fireflies. She felt the light within herself and leant against the stone cross, touching the sunken ring of stone that somehow held light.

"All substance is tones of light," she whispered. A blackbird started its song to the fading day.

She was reluctant to leave when Vladimir called her but he was worried about the journey back. She lingered by the old gateway, trying to paint the image of the place in her mind.

"Why did you come to Ireland Vladimir?" she asked him as they motored along the darkening road.

"Because my wife was an Irish girl. And I came over here to meet her family and just stayed."

"I didn't know priests could marry."

"Well, we have a choice before we become priests whether to be monastics or to marry. Alexei, my friend, he chose the monastic life but I knew that I should want a wife. I met Mary in France during the war. She was a teacher. She taught me all the English I know."

"What happened to her? Is she still alive?"

"Unfortunately, no. She died in nineteen sixty."

Sophie did not press him further on the subject and they

continued in silence for the rest of the journey, Sophie trying to imagine what kind of woman his wife had been and presuming that in the silence his memories were of the time shared with her. Just before they reached De Courcy House he spoke again.

"Not many people understand that the Russian Orthodox is very different. My mother became a nun and my father and grandfather were priests."

"Really," Sophie said. She asked him quickly, just as he was leaving her and then wondered why she had asked the question.

"Vladimir, could a divorced woman become a nun?"

"Yes," he replied with a smile, "if God willed it."

It was three weeks of talking to her, caring for her and filling her days, before the old Gloria that Sophie loved reappeared. Her speech was slower as if the lost personality had to struggle to make itself known. She had been like a child having to learn the fundamental art of living again. She was full of remorse, shame and confusion about Steve's death. She would blame herself for not being more attentive to him and then escape the reality of her past actions by incessant, trivial gossip. Depressions were followed by periods of self-loathing during which Sophie would do her best to build up the sick woman's confidence.

Eventually she asked Sophie, "Did anyone know I was doped out of my eyeballs at the funeral?"

"No," Sophie lied, "I think they just thought you were shocked and upset."

This seemed to reassure her and she asked Michael to drive her to the graveyard so she could be alone with Steve. She returned after an hour and walked around the garden with Sophie and the dogs.

"I want to be buried with Steve when I die Sophie." She

began to weep and Sophie consoled her. "God knows what I ever did to deserve that man. He was a damned saint."

She wanted to talk about him. About their life together and retell all the best times they'd ever had. Sophie noticed that when she talked of the past, her happy memories always included a comment on the quantity of drugs or booze that she was consuming at the time. Sophie realised that apart from the times they had spent together, when they first met, on holiday in Tunisia or during the brief sojourns at the Ritz, Gloria's entire view of life had been influenced by drugs. Often Sophie would try to change the direction of her thoughts by steering the conversation away from her drug associations but Gloria would always skilfully manoeuvre the subject back to a drug-related incident.

The nurse only called twice a week now and Maureen and Sophie looked after and administered the pills. When the nurse spent the day with Gloria, Sophie would visit Vladimir. There was so much he wanted to show her and share with her. They would sit talking for hours or walk in the country-side, lunching by lakes or on hills where there was no sound but the soft footfall of sheep or the scuffling of birds. He introduced her to a world of gently humorous people with clear, honest eyes whereas the more she spoke to Gloria about her life in Dublin, it appeared that since they had both first met a web of poisonous drug pushing had spread through the city.

"But," she protested one day after listening to one of Gloria's reminiscences, "when I saw you in New York, you were off it weren't you?"

"No dear, I was juggling them then. You know when I got back, they had to carry me off the plane I was so bombed."

"I didn't realise."

"Well, we thought it was best you didn't know."

"But why Gloria? Why couldn't you share that with me? I'm supposed to be your friend."

"Well, to be honest dear, I guess I was scared about the effect it might have on you. After all, I had sort of sponsored your recovery and besides, I think Steve told me not to worry you."

Sophie wondered whether this was the truth or whether it was as Steve had once told her, that Gloria had gauged how much she could get away with, by Sophie's ignorance. It was unimportant she decided. At least she was trying to be honest now.

After a phone call from Jacob telling her about tickets and arrangements for France and her new film, she returned to the lounge to find Gloria miserable and forlorn.

"Sophie, I just can't stay here on my own. Everything reminds me of Steve and I know I'm too weak. I know me. I know I'll go back on it. I've just got to go somewhere."

"Do you want to move to London where you'll be near me?"

"Gee that would be great. Would you help me find an apartment?"

"Of course I will."

"But first Sophie, I've got to go to the places Steve and I talked about. We used to plan this trip around the world. I've got the maps we looked at upstairs and all the brochures. God, how I wish I hadn't put things off. I wish we'd gone when he was alive. I feel I've got to go and see them now, for him. You understand don't you?"

"Yes but do you think you could cope with travel so soon after all this? And if you want to go around the world, it needs careful planning."

"I've got to go Sophie. Could you come with me?"

"Well not now Gloria. I should really have gone back to London sooner and the latest I can leave it is Saturday. I've got to get everything ready for France. I'm there until July."

"Can't you get out of it?" Gloria looked at her with pleading eyes and Sophie felt mean.

"Gloria, I'm sorry but I've signed a contract. They can sue me if I just don't turn up."

"Then I'll have to go on my own." Her shoulders slumped with disappointment and she sat looking little and alone. Sophie searched for an answer, feeling wretched at Gloria's deflated appearance. She heard Maureen bustling about the kitchen and found her idea.

"Gloria, why don't you take Maureen? Think how much it would mean to her. She's never been out of Ireland. She would be able to see places that she could never afford to visit."

Gloria looked dubious.

"Think Gloria. You give to art funding so that people have a chance to see beautiful pictures. Why not invest in a wonderful experience for someone who has looked after you. I think Steve would approve."

"Yeah, Steve always said Maureen was great with us." Gloria was thoughtful. "And she could look after things, couldn't she?"

"She would remember you and the trip for the rest of her life. You and I have travelled but Maureen would have to win the pools to get such an opportunity."

Gloria's face softened. "I guess it really would be something for her wouldn't it? Will you ask her for me?"

"No, I think you should."

"What if she says no?"

"I don't think she will but you're not going to find out unless you ask."

The shriek from the kitchen told Sophie the answer. Maureen was terrified and thrilled at the same time. "Oh

187

Sophie, oh Sophie, me going round the world. Wait till I tell my friends, they'll be green. I think I'll buy one of those new trouser suits I've seen. Say I meet someone nice. What about that? Well, it's possible isn't it?"

By the time Sophie had to leave for London, De Courcy House was full of energy and optimism as the two women planned the trip, their wardrobes and the length of time to be spent in each country. They promised to send cards from every place visited and Maureen swore that she would protect Gloria with her life. Vladimir came to the airport to say goodbye.

"While you are in France, see if you can visit Maison des Sœurs, Bussy-en-Othe. It is a small monastery and they are friends of mine. They would make you very welcome."

"I'll try." She hugged him as she left but in the plane later, she felt that she never really said goodbye to Vladimir because somehow he always seemed to be at her side. Like an inspiring shadow.

Chapter Eleven

It was late February, nineteen seventy-three, when Sophie arrived home. She had been travelling for almost twenty-four hours with a delay of eight hours in Nairobi airport. The small hallway was littered with postcards from exotic places. She stepped over them wearily. They could be sorted into chronological order later. All she wanted now, was to drink tea made with English milk and to soak in a bath without the fear of anything crawling out of anywhere. Sod's law had decreed that while Gloria and Maureen toured the exciting, romantic places in the world, she had been filming in the rain forests of Brazil and the deserts of Namibia.

Shortly after she had left Ireland to film in France, Bob Cantor had taken over the agency. Jacob had told her that he was a hustler. That had been an understatement. Within weeks, she had contracts for two more films, each one overlapping the other. There was no time to visit Vladimir's friends at the monastery. All her free days were either spent in Paris or London, talking to producers, fitting clothes or testing make-up. Now, after nine months' continual work, she wanted to sleep with the knowledge that there was no time limit on her freedom.

The sound of sleet pattering against the windows woke her. She lay contentedly listening to the familiar sounds of passing traffic and the usual movements within Nell Gwynn House. After only a few hours' rest, she was surprisingly alert. She heated up some tinned soup and began sifting through Gloria's and Maureen's cards and letters. On one of her trips from France she had collected their first batch of letters, all giving lengthy descriptions of their adventures and travels. As their journey round the world continued their messages became briefer. Most of Gloria's cards had either "Get a load of this" or "Having a ball in . . ." on the back of a picture of the hotel in which they were staying. Maureen always sent a card with a beautiful view and a reassuring postscript that "Gloria's fine", "Gloria's doing well", or "Gloria seems to be fine".

Then Gloria posted a letter from Jamaica complaining that Maureen had "gone wild in the Caribbean". A Canadian had apparently joined the luxury liner that was touring the islands. "This guy," she wrote, "is the son of Irish immigrants and like all Irishmen has waited as long as possible before thinking of marriage. I think Maureen reminds him of his mother. Well dear, she has flipped her clogs . . ." A letter posted the same week from Maureen contained two pages about the wonderful Canadian called Sean. He was going to come to Dublin after Gloria had moved to London and they were to be married. Then they would leave for Canada. "How strange, Sophie," she wrote, "that I have to come all the way here to meet the man of my dreams." Sophie hoped the Canadian would keep all his promises and not let Maureen down. The postscript said, "I think Gloria's having the odd nip of booze. I'm not sure and I haven't found any bottles in her cabin but I think she's got the steward well trained. I think she's fine though."

The final letter in the pile was posted from Dublin in January. Gloria's scrawl said that she was going to be at the Ritz from March the first and had arranged a birthday tea for the third, in memory of Steve's birthday. She hoped Sophie would be back in time for it.

Sophie checked her watch. It was eleven-thirty. Gloria was bound still to be awake. She dialled for the operator with a certain degree of apprehension. Hopefully, Maureen was right and Gloria was still "fine".

"Darling. How are you? Where have you been, Sophie?"

It was lovely to hear her dirty laugh when she was told of the indignities of filming in such primitive locations. They gossiped for hours, giggling over the ridiculous stories and commiserating with each other's dramas.

"Dear, when I come over, I'm going to look for an apartment near to your place. Will you help me? Do you have the time?"

"I don't want to work for ages, Gloria. Of course I'll help."

"The amount of rent I've paid this dame, I could have bought the damn place ten times over. Wait till you see what I got in Hong Kong for your birthday."

"And wait till you see what I've brought you from Africa." The telephone line crackled as they both shrieked with laughter.

"Gloria, do you want to go and see *Applause*? If you like I'll get tickets."

"Tea and then the theatre. That sounds great dear. And we'll have dinner at the Ritz afterwards."

"Well, see how we feel after that huge tea."

"You're right. We'll play it by ear. I can't wait to see you dear."

"And how's Maureen?"

"Well, the letters arrive daily. She's mooching around like a love sick calf, just waiting for me to be gone so he'll come over and take her back with him. To be fair. He's not a bad guy dear. She could have done a whole lot worse."

No one has to follow an inevitable course of self-destruction, Sophie thought as she replaced the receiver.

Anyone can change their direction in life. All it needs is one moment of honest decision. She thanked God that Gloria had made that decision.

The birthday cake was a chocolate shark. It had two candles wedged against each side of the triangular fin.

"He used to love to try and catch sharks off the Cork coast," Gloria said. "He caught a tiny one once and he was so excited. The thing was so sleepy, you'd have thought it was stoned." She laughed. "Sophie, it gave one flip and just lay there. I've got a snapshot somewhere at home of Steve holding it up."

There was peppermint cream in between the layers of chocolate sponge. The two women munched the cake reverently as they remembered Steve.

"Did I tell you I was searched in Harrods?" Gloria said. "They're really taking this IRA thing seriously. I had no idea how bad it was here."

"I've heard there've been quite a few scares," Sophie said. "There's a strange feeling in London. It's almost like we've come to the end of an era. There's an angry, watchful mood. You can sense it."

"I think I've found a flat in Eaton Square," Gloria said. "Am I right in thinking that's not far from you?"

"Only five minutes' walk. Have you seen it yet?"

"No. I believe the guy's coming to get me tomorrow. About midday. He says there's a park or something where I can walk the dogs. Are you nearly finished? Because I want to show you what I'm wearing tonight. I've got a marvellous knitted, three-piece outfit by Cyril Cullen. I bought it last year and never wore it. I thought it would be perfect for the theatre."

Sophie's shoulders drooped. She would have to return to the flat and change if Gloria was going to dress up for the evening.

"Would you like the rest of the cake sent up to your suite, Mrs O'Connell?" the head waiter asked her.

"Well I don't know," Gloria said. "Would you like to take it home with you Sophie?"

"Yes please."

"Michael, could you wrap it for Sophie?"

"Certainly."

"Oh, and while we're here. Next year we'll have the birthday on the nineteenth of February. Your birthday dear," Gloria said. "What sort of cake shall we have for Sophie, Michael?"

Michael smiled. "Would a starfish be appropriate?"

"Great." Gloria's yell of approval reverberated through the Palm Court.

It looked as if a tornado had hit her suite. Clothes and tissues were strewn everywhere.

"Let me show you what I brought back for you, some little mementoes from the trip. And the most important thing, your birthday present."

"And I've got yours." Sophie pulled two packages out of her bag and gave them to Gloria.

"Look dear, these are yours." Sophie saw little wicker baskets, scarfs and a collection of shells and corals. She picked up a large shell and listened to the sound of the sea. "That one's the birthday present." Gloria pointed excitedly to a small parcel wrapped in silver paper. Sophie unwrapped it. Inside, lying on raw cotton wool, was a malachite crucifix with a diamond in the centre. "Do you like it?" Gloria asked. "I found it in Hong Kong."

"I love it. It's beautiful," Sophie gasped. Gloria's face flushed with pleasure.

"But you must open yours Gloria."

Gloria unwrapped the big one first and let out a yell. "What's this?"

Sophie was giggling. "It's an African fertility mask."

"Ah." Gloria danced about holding the wooden face in front of her. "I'll use it to scare away burglars. Wait till the dogs see it, they'll go wild."

"Now open this one," Sophie said.

Gloria found the gold and ivory bracelet and cooed happily. "Oh dear, this is wonderful. Look, it matches my Cyril Cullen outfit. I'll wear it tonight.

"Ah, about tonight," Sophie said. "Look, I'll have to go home and change if you're wearing that. I'll pick you up at the Arlington Street entrance at seven. Okay?"

"Right dear." Gloria looked uncertain. "I don't have to change if you'd rather . . ."

"No, it's okay. Your outfit will look stunning on you and it's good for me to make some effort. See you later."

"Don't forget to collect the cake from Michael," Gloria shouted after her.

Sophie knew that if she told her to be ready for seven, Gloria would arrive downstairs at seven fifteen. It was in her nature to be late. But at least they would be in time for the theatre. As she changed, something about Gloria began to bother her. It wasn't the fact that the twitch on the left side of Gloria's face was more pronounced. Her speech was quicker now, not slurred as it had been before. She couldn't think what it was. When she collected her from the Ritz, the answer was staring her in the face. Gloria had begun wearing dark glasses again. She had put on jewelled ones for the evening and she looked very attractive but Sophie wondered why she felt the need to hide behind them.

"You look wonderful Gloria. It really is a super outfit."

"Thank you dear. And you look pretty glamorous yourself. What is that? Crochet?"

"I think so. I was given it when Vogue did that article last year," Sophie said. "Can you see all right in your glasses?"

"Oh yes," Gloria said. "The light hurts my eyes sometimes. Especially those neon lights." Sophie tried to believe her.

The choice of show had been a good one. Gloria enjoyed it enormously, laughing loudly at the humour and nudging Sophie's arm when she agreed with anything said. During the interval she stood watching the people in the bar and smoking while Sophie struggled through the crowd at the counter in an attempt to buy some fruit juice. After several minutes she emerged triumphantly carrying two smeared glasses to find Gloria poised like a cat watching a bird. She looked in the direction of her gaze and spotted Sebastian Fielding, a tall good looking actor. She had often seen him at the odd film party, usually escorting older, famous actresses. When he accompanied them, he wore very conservative clothes. Now, he was dressed more flamboyantly. His eyes searched the crowded bar for a friendly look and found Gloria's jewelled sunglasses focused on him. He smiled and sidled over towards them.

"Hello Sophie." He enunciated beautifully, pronouncing Sophie as if it were So Fair. Sophie could smell the mouthwash.

"Gloria, this is Sebastian Fielding. Sebastian, Gloria O'Connell."

"How do you do, Gloria. May I say how charming your outfit looks."

Gloria purred into conversation. As she fumbled with a packet of Gauloises, he produced an expensive cigarette lighter and stood attentively listening, gas burning, while she talked and measured the distance between the flame and the end of her cigarette. Sophie watched the strange mating dance during which Sebastian charmed Gloria and Gloria intrigued him. Whenever Sophie had met him before, he was always just finishing or about to begin, a nostalgic provincial tour playing opposite the current older actress of the time.

"Are you working, Sebastian?" she asked him. He was saved by the bell. He relieved them of their glasses and insisted on escorting them to their seats. Gloria's neck nearly twisted off watching him walk back up the aisle.

"Now that is one hell of a lovely guy," she said. Sophie was silent. "Is he famous, Sophie?"

"No."

"But I'll bet he's a good actor isn't he?"

"I don't know. I've never seen his work."

"Is he married?"

"I don't think so."

"Fancy that. And he's such a handsome guy. He's not a fag, is he?"

"I've no idea Gloria. I hardly know him."

At the end of the show, Gloria looked for Sebastian in the foyer. He was near the doors talking to some people. He glanced towards her and his smile was all the encouragement she needed. Dragging a reluctant Sophie by the arm, she made her way to him. After they had exchanged a few words about the show, Sophie announced that it was time for them to leave. As he opened the door for them, Gloria saw the dark shadow of impending stubble and her stomach kicked. It was like Steve's predawn look when they'd first met at her deb party. She found herself asking Sebastian whether he would like to join them at the Ritz for coffee and sandwiches. Sophie, she noticed, had the same glowering scowl that she'd once seen in Tunisia. Gloria wondered whether she was jealous of all the attention Sebastian paid her. When he helped them into the taxi, he gave Gloria's arm a squeeze and she knew an affair was in the offing.

Sophie was unable to eat any more sandwiches or to drink any more coffee. She felt very much in the way of the budding romance. She had tried to talk to Sebastian about his past work but all he wanted to discuss was the musical he'd written. It sounded to Sophie like a banal load of rubbish but Gloria went on about how she adored musicals and listed all the great Broadway shows she'd seen. Sophie could almost hear Steve whispering from beyond the grave, "This year Sophie, it's musicals." She watched Gloria's movements towards him become more tactile, so she made her excuses, lying about an early morning appointment and left. After all, it was now after midnight and Steve's birthday was over.

As Sophie walked away, Sebastian let out a sigh of relief. He visibly relaxed and the twinkle in his eye again reassured Gloria that it was her company that he found attractive. They talked until two in the morning. He told her about his life in the theatre and how his family had not approved of his chosen career. He was an ex-public schoolboy, he explained, and had been expected to follow his father's footsteps in law. He hinted that there was a title in the family.

Gloria told him about her family background and he listened most attentively. They had a lot in common, he pointed out and referred to "People with our upbringing" or "People like us". He became more and more attractive as they talked. She thought he was amusing, eloquent and had well-manicured hands. As he was leaving, he asked whether he could accompany her when she viewed the Eaton Square apartment. Perhaps she would care to have lunch with him afterwards. When he said goodnight, he kissed her hand and she floated up to her suite, glowing with excitement. Later, she smoked a joint and wondered when they would make love.

When Sophie telephoned the Ritz the next day, she was told that Mrs O'Connell was out and not expected back until late. She left a message but three days passed before Gloria returned her call.

"Sophie guess what?" she shouted. "I've taken an

apartment in Eaton Square. I've been out with Sebastian to meet this designer who's in films and we've been arranging colours and furniture and everything. And Sebastian knows this place where you can hire very high class staff."

"I'd love to see the flat, Gloria," Sophie said.

"I can't take you there today dear. Philip, that's Sebastian's designer friend, well, he's got the keys, for all the designing. He says it will be ready in a couple of months."

"Do you want to have lunch, Gloria?"

"Darling, I can't. I have a hair appointment. But we could have tea here, say about four?"

Gloria sat looking bright and sparkling. She was not wearing her sunglasses and her eyes watched Sophie's reactions with excited expectancy. Having told Sophie all about the past three days with Sebastian, she was waiting for a comment on her news, some approval of her new relationship. Sophie, aware that Gloria was smitten with the man, tried to choose her words carefully. In no way did she want to undermine her friend's new, bubbling self-confidence but she had to warn her. She started gently to explain about his reputation. Gloria tilted her head to one side and smiled knowingly.

"Let's face it dear. Don't you think perhaps you might be just a little prejudiced? After all, your man is not the usual type of actor, is he? I mean with his kind of background."

Sophie frowned. "I don't know what you mean."

Gloria watched the expression on Sophie's face. She was reacting in the exact way that Sebastian had said she would. He had explained to her that often actors from the working or the lower middle classes, resented his type of person. He had said that Gloria of all people should understand how difficult it was to be accepted when one came from a privileged background. She had argued that Sophie thought quite differently. But he insisted that the class system in

England was something that an American could never understand.

"I don't want you to be hurt," Sophie was saying, "and he's a dreadful smoothie. Take everything he says with a great big pinch of salt." Sophie was reluctant to spell it out too cruelly. She could not bring herself to say that it was Gloria's money that Sebastian was after. That he was a gigolo of the worst kind, adapting like a chameleon to every rich woman he wooed.

"Just don't get too involved with him Gloria," Sophie said.

Gloria felt irritated that Sophie's words had filled her with doubt. The possibility of being deprived of the romance and his sensual, communicating hands, was too painful to think about. She straightened her back and lit a cigarette.

"Sophie dear, I'm not a fool but I do like a man around me." She silenced Sophie's attempts to speak. "Okay, so he's smooth but he's very sweet and very sexy, Sophie, he really has some very nice ways. And he's helped me to get to know people. It's very hard Sophie to go out in London without a man."

Sophie looked at Gloria's small face. Her eyes were full of reproof. She shrugged her shoulders. "Well, you've certainly got one of the best escorts in town," she said. "But Gloria, he's not a Steve. I just don't want you to think he is."

Gloria's eyes became brilliant with anger. She began to blink and the frequency of her facial twitch increased. Sophie knew she had gone too far and immediately regretted it.

"I don't want to talk about him any more," Gloria said. "I really think my personal life is up to me. After all dear, you're hardly the expert on fellows are you?"

Sophie was silent. Gloria was right. Who the hell was she to interfere. Gloria was puffing her cigarette furiously. When she spoke her voice croaked with emotion.

"Celibacy is very unhealthy," she said. "Just because

you're frigid, it does not give you the right to criticise me for being a normal, healthy woman."

Sophie was wounded and felt close to tears. She had been fighting on Gloria's side but was now completely out of the battle. She retreated into politeness. The rest of the tea was finished in silence. Gloria's last words to her as she left were, "There'll be a housewarming when I move into Eaton Square. I'll let you know when it is."

Sophie nodded. The gate had been left open for their friendship.

Sophie walked along Piccadilly. She knew she could never explain to Gloria that she did love deeply but she found emotionalism always took something away from her, whereas detachment allowed her to love that which was within someone rather than just their external personality. She felt sad that Gloria was incapable of understanding the joy she found from the intensely personal relationship with the Master and his overshadowing. "Many young priests who daily fight the passions of a carnal nature, would probably think of you as being blessed in having that urge removed Sophie," Vladimir had said. "But ask yourself honestly. Whether it is fear of love or not wishing to give or share love, that is your truth?"

Since talking it over with Vladimir, she had asked herself that question continually. While in Africa, working mostly with men, she had been friendly and loving. There had been the occasional reassuring cuddle when faced with some difficult scene. The primitive countryside had resounded with the rhythm of sex and the urgent need for reproduction but she knew she had no desire to take part. It was not her truth.

*

When Gloria arrived back at De Courcy House, the weather had turned colder. The ground had become hard and was covered with a layer of frost. The whole place had a desolate feeling as if knowing she was about to leave. The dogs followed her everywhere, suspicious of her movements. Maureen was in a world of her own, preoccupied with all the packing and constantly reading Sean's letters. She hardly mentioned Gloria's trip to London apart from asking after Sophie. Gloria visited Steve's grave but it was too cold to stay long. It was with relief that she climbed back into the warmth of the Mercedes. Only two days had passed and London seemed like a dream away. She felt guilty about the row with Sophie. After all, the girl was probably just being loyal to Steve, like a child, Gloria thought.

Sebastian telephoned that evening. "I don't want you to think I've forgotten you," he said softly. And then with a catch in his breath, he said, "If I saw you at the moment, I'd say why am I here and she's there. I just can't handle it at the moment. I'm trying to pull myself together."

The conversation became more sensual. He made her feel so young and so desirable that she wanted to reach down the telephone wire and haul him through. She spent her days in and out of sexual fantasies. The telephone conversations had become more and more explicit, so that she was overwhelmed by desire. At last she decided she had to telephone Sophie and was happy to hear the relief in the girl's voice when she answered.

"Sophie, isn't it sad about Picasso?" Gloria said. "It's on the front pages of the *Irish Times*. Did I ever tell you I met him once in Paris?"

"No," Sophie said. "I once read a story about this couple who watched him or somebody like him, on the beach drawing a picture in the sand. And they went off for spades to dig it up but when they returned, the tide had washed it away. I don't know why I always remember that story."

"How are you dear?"

"Well, it looks as if I'll be spending the summer filming in the Orkneys." She explained to Gloria where the Orkneys were.

"Did I ever tell you that some of my ancestors were Scotch." Gloria said and launched into a history of her family tree. By the time they had finished gossiping, all tension between them had vanished.

"I'm sorry I was insensitive, Gloria," Sophie said.

Gloria felt magnanimous. "Not to worry dear. I really shouldn't have reacted like I did."

Each night Sebastian called her. First he would tell her news about the flat and then he would woo her with the language of love. By the third week in May, the decorating was completed. When the time came for her to leave, Maureen cried uncontrollably. Gloria was surprised that the woman had so much feeling for her. Instead of selling the Mercedes, Gloria had given it to Michael as a bonus for his past services. As there was a twenty-four hour taxi strike in Dublin on the day she left, her generosity reaped its rewards. He returned from his home in Wicklow to take her to the airport. She was met at Heathrow by Sebastian who had brought a Fortnum and Mason hamper so that they could picnic in style in the new apartment.

The designer had created a world of soft mushroom and pinks. The windows were draped in curtains of pink and cream satin. When she walked into her dressing room, the lighting was soft so that despite the tiredness from her journey, she looked attractive. The whole effect was like walking in a soft carpeted, pink shell. They smoked grass together before making love and he left discreetly before dawn. He helped her to plan the housewarming by organising the catering and staff.

"He's great in the feathers," she confided in Sophie as they talked in a corner away from the rest of the party.

Sophie watched the glow of pleasure on her friend's face and wondered whether she had misjudged Sebastian. Perhaps, like many other people's characters in show business, his had been tarnished by unfounded gossip. He was certainly being a discreet lover and for that Sophie was grateful. She would have hated Gloria to be made a figure of fun in the gossip columns. Gloria had become so confident but there was something about the way Sebastian's eyes shifted when Sophie looked at him that still made her feel uneasy.

*

The film set in the Orkneys was a low budget movie. After six weeks filming in Orkney, she was flown to Edinburgh with some other actors, for a three day break in which time she would be able to see the start of the festival before returning to work for a further four weeks. It was good to be back in a city listening to the noises of traffic and bustling sounds of people in the streets after such a long time on an island. She had been booked into the Caledonian and revelled in the joys of room service and her own bathroom. It was quite by chance that she found out about the wedding. Her breakfast had been delivered with a morning paper. There on the third page was a picture of Sebastian and Gloria surrounded by grinning faces, in front of the Caxton Hall registry office. The caption said, "Mr and Mrs Fielding will honeymoon at the Marbella Club for two weeks before returning for the rehearsals of his new musical which opens in October." Apparently Gloria had described the musical as being the best since *Oklahoma* which was why she was backing it.

Sophie was stunned. As soon as she had first arrived in Kirkwall, the main town in Orkney, she had telephoned Gloria. A housekeeper had answered. Sophie had been told that Mrs O'Connell was not in but that her message would be passed on with her telephone number. After several days, there had still been no response. Sophie continued to call and leave messages and checked and double checked that Gloria had not returned her call. If she had known her friend was getting married, she would have moved heaven and hell to be with her on the day. Later, walking along Princes Street in a state of confusion, the sound of two women giggling at a street performer, started off the pain and anguish. An aching loneliness and a feeling of betrayal forced her to find a quiet corner where she could let the tears flow freely. She made the effort to climb the Mound and wandered down alleyways and twittens, fighting to find reasons or excuses for Gloria's silence. At the end of the unhappy day, she sent a telegram of congratulations to the couple and reminded them that she would be returning to London in September.

It was late September before she finished the film. After trying unsuccessfully several times to contact Gloria, she bought a wedding present and posted it to her. She received a polite thank you card signed by Sebastian. Sophie became worried. Gloria would never be rude. The silence was extremely suspicious. She wondered whether she was back on drugs again and if so, whether Sebastian was looking after her properly. She kept telephoning and leaving messages.

"Do you want to come with us to this extraordinary first night, Sophie?" Bob Cantor did not know she was Gloria's friend. "A few of us from the office are going, to give our client some moral support. I tell you, it's had more money spent on publicity than any other show I can remember. It's got to be the biggest joke of the season." He roared with laughter. "This rich woman backer has paid for the best director and the best cast and for the worst load of trash ever written. She must be mad or Sebastian Fielding is the best stud in town. Believe me Sophie, our client is getting a fortune but I'm negotiating his next show now. If this thing lasts two nights it will be a miracle. Why don't you come. It will be a laugh. We're all going to the Ivy for dinner afterwards."

"Where shall I meet you Bob?"

"I'll pick you up at your place at six thirty."

From her position inside the crowded foyer, Sophie saw Gloria arrive in a chauffeur-driven white Rolls Royce. Sebastian held her firmly by the arm. On his other side, hanging on to his shoulder was an old girlfriend, an ex-nightclub hostess who had been named in a government sex scandal. Sophie bit her lip. Gloria looked like a fairy queen. Her dress was covered in spangles and sequins and she was wearing a glittering tiara on her head. All around her, Sophie could hear people making whispered innuendoes and sniggering behind programmes. Gloria's eyes were dazed as she lurched along the carpeted path to the theatre. Once inside, she was guided through the scrum towards a private bar where a group of Sebastian's friends were having a pre-performance drink.

Bob Cantor's seats were in the front row of the Royal Circle. Sophie could see Gloria in her box. She was just staring down at the orchestra. The show was dreadful but brilliantly executed. It was a mixture of several styles varying between Sandy Wilson, Coward and Cole Porter. One song began like *Night and Day* and ended with the words "And her father came too". Laughter greeted all the serious moments in the story and the jokes were received with groans. Out of the corner of her eye, Sophie saw Gloria noisily vacate her seat in the box. Sophie immediately left her seat and rushed to the nearest lavatory in Gloria's vicinity. Sophie's hunch was correct. Gloria crashed her way in, followed closely by Sebastian's ex-girlfriend.

"Sophie, where have you been?" Gloria hugged her. The other woman looked uneasy.

"I've tried to see you Gloria," Sophie said. "Didn't you get my messages or the wedding present I sent you?"

"No dear. Wait a minute, I've just got to go." She disappeared into a cubicle. The other woman hovered round the wash basin, powdering her face and combing her hair. After a lot of clattering and swearing, Gloria emerged.

"But I wanted you to come to the wedding darling and no one knew where you were."

"I think we should go back in now Gloria." Sebastian's girlfriend went to take her arm.

"No, you go back. I've seen it a hundred times. I want to talk to Sophie."

"But I don't think Sebastian would like that . . ." The woman looked worried.

"I'll be in later," Gloria said. The woman hurried out. Gloria stood looking confused. "You left messages? But I never got them. I was very hurt, Sophie, I thought it was because you didn't like Sebastian."

"Gloria, I read about your wedding and I was hurt. I'd been leaving messages for weeks."

Gloria's expression was that of fear and bewilderment. "I just don't understand," she said.

"Listen Gloria, I'm home now. You can phone me. And if that's impossible, remember we're meeting at the Ritz for our tea in February. The nineteenth. Can you remember that?"

"But of course. I'll phone you. I'll throw a party for you."

"No Gloria, I don't want a party. I just want to know how you are. Are you happy?"

Gloria became uncertain and hesitant. "Well dear, he's not like Steve but really I'm very lucky to have married again. He's got a few hang-ups and he's very possessive but I suppose that's the way Englishmen are."

As Sophie had anticipated, the door to the ladies' room

burst open and Sebastian and his woman friend walked in.

"For God's sake, Gloria," he said, "what are you doing in the ladies' lavatory when you're meant to be watching the show?"

"Sophie's here and I haven't seen her for ages."

"Well you can talk to her later. What do you think the gossip writers will say when my own wife doesn't sit through the performance?"

Gloria had become a meek and frightened mouse. Sophie watched the scene with distaste. As Sebastian pushed Gloria out of the door, Sophie tapped him on the arm. "I hope you get all the success you deserve," she said.

The critics slammed the show. It was joked about on radio discussion programmes and comedians were guaranteed a laugh from any television audience when referring to it. Despite the rumours suggesting that Gloria would nurse the show, it came off in six weeks. Sophie waited until the end of November before she called Gloria again. She half expected the usual excuses from the housekeeper but this time Sebastian was brought to the telephone. Sophie was completely thrown by his charming manner. "Why don't you come round Sophie, for a drink. Shall we say six?"

Sophie arrived promptly at six. She was surprised when Sebastian, dressed in a velvet smoking jacket, answered the door and took her coat. She had been expecting to see the housekeeper. Many exquisite antiques had been added to the flat since the housewarming. Sebastian led her towards the large Adam fireplace where Gloria sat propped up by cushions in an elegant Victorian chair. Sophie felt utter despair when she saw her. Gloria's eyes were drooping and her head lolled about.

"Hello Sophie." The words dragged themselves from her lips.

"What would you like to drink Sophie?" Sebastian asked in the best drawing room comedy manner.

"Fruit juice please."

"Oh dear. I'm afraid we haven't any. Would anything else do? Gloria likes Pimms. Can I make you one?"

"No," Gloria croaked.

"No thank you. I'll have plain tap water," Sophie said.

"What very simple tastes."

Sophie knelt down and hugged Gloria.

"Sophie."

"Yes."

"I've missed you."

Sebastian returned and began to make small talk. Gloria occasionally managed to say something vague. Every word she uttered was a long drawn out effort on the same flat note. Sophie noticed that Sebastian didn't light Gloria's cigarettes any more. The drugged woman took an age to get one out of the packet and spilled most of them on to the carpet. Sebastian ignored her efforts as if she were an ill-mannered animal. Sophie reached for the table lighter.

"Thank you Sophie," Gloria whispered.

Sophie took Gloria's free hand and rubbed it, trying to infuse some of her own will power into Gloria's being.

"Why Sophie," Sebastian quipped, "I didn't realise you were that way."

Sophie felt sick and for the first time in her life understood the spontaneous emotion that led to murder. He stood looking at her mockingly.

"I'm afraid I have to go," she said clenching her fists with anger.

"Must you?" he said.

"Yes." She glared at him. "Please could I have my coat?" She waited until he was out of earshot and bent down and whispered to Gloria: "See you at the Ritz."

"What's that? We can't have secrets." Sebastian was smirking by the door.

As Sophie left, Gloria was nodding to herself.

All Sophie could do was to pray and hope. She checked with Michael that they could have the starfish with two candles and she arrived early just in case Gloria was confused when she turned up. The tiny, bizarre figure was already there, sitting alone in the corner. Her hair was coloured a bright maroon and she was wearing enormous sunglasses. Sophie nearly squeezed the breath out of her.

"Does he know you're here?" she asked.

"No." Gloria was wheezing badly. Sophie noticed for the first time she was without the little silver fish.

"Where's your fish?" she said.

"I broke it on the honeymoon. But dear, it was a bit hectic at the time." They both laughed.

"Oh," Gloria said wistfully, "it's like old times."

"Are you still happy with him?"

"I think he's a bit mixed up dear. He's very insecure but he has a very sweet side. Of course I'm older than him."

She changed the subject and started to talk about the past with more fervour. Sophie kept trying to get her to share any problems with her but Gloria avoided facing any unpleasant reality. Throughout the tea, she checked her watch nervously. As they were leaving, Sophie noticed the dark bruising by the edge of the sunglasses.

"Has he ever hit you Gloria?" she asked.

Gloria paused too long for Sophie to believe the denial.

"It will be on my birthday next year," Gloria said. "The thirteenth of March. It will be our fifth birthday together. Perhaps we ought to arrange it now?"

"Leave it to me," Sophie said. "I'll fix it all. Please Gloria, if you ever need any help or anything, call me."

Gloria climbed awkwardly into the taxi and then clutched Sophie's hand.

"Sophie, I'm weak," she said. "I've tried . . . I've tried so many times but you know I keep slipping."

"Gloria, you can try again," Sophie said. "You can start a new day. Why don't you go into a clinic?"

"I can't do it Sophie," Gloria said, "but you did it. I'm so proud of you. You can do it. Do it for me too. I love you Sophie. I love you the best."

Sophie watched the taxi pull away. She felt like the last runner in a relay. Gloria and Steve had given her a torch, Vladimir had lit it and she knew she had to reach some goal for all of them.

Chapter Twelve

The telephone calls were always late at night when Sebastian had gone out and Gloria felt lonely. Sophie waited for them with a mixture of longing and dread. A part of her hoped for a miracle—hoped that one day Gloria would say, "Sophie, I'm ready to go into a clinic now." But the voice on the line would be incoherent, slurred and rambling and Sophie would spend a fretful night wondering what she could possibly do to help her friend.

Providing that she was not working the next day, she could cope with the calls. But when she had an early start in the studio or on location, they robbed her of vital sleep. The film she was making was about a group of nuns caught up in the Inquisition. The atmosphere in the studio was heavy and depressing. The combination of the strange drama enacted during the day and the endless late-night telephone calls began to take its toll. She questioned her own faith and the reasons for pain and suffering. She thrashed about in her mind, drowning in the world's sorrows. On her days off, she found herself weeping as she walked past marching strikers in the streets. She was confused by the angry graffiti that was appearing on walls and she raged when she saw young boys and girls around Piccadilly selling their youth for a fix. Her work became a reflection of the heresy in society. Her past yearning and striving for the light was forgotten as the despair and darkness engulfed her. And the late-night calls continued with Gloria's hoarse voice croaking out her loneliness.

Vladimir kept writing to her suggesting that meditation might help while she was under so much pressure. He then sent her an icon and story about Saint Seraphim, one of the great Russian Saints. He had been a staretz, a priest monk, whose spiritual discernment and wisdom inspired both monks and lay people to come to him for guidance. Comforted by the story, Sophie began to pray again.

There was a lull in the disturbing late-night calls and during the calm she experienced a change in awareness. It happened suddenly one afternoon when she was working on location in some woods. It was like waking up to a new dimension of being. She remembered Vladimir's story of the dragonfly shedding its old form and preparing for a new life and her heart felt free for the first time for months. She continued to pray daily for Gloria.

Later in the autumn, what seemed like the longed-for miracle happened. Without any warning Gloria rang late one night and asked for help. She sounded frightened and said she wanted to go into a clinic. Sophie had already consulted a doctor specialising in addiction and he had told her that Gloria could come into his clinic at any time of day or night. Sophie rushed round to Gloria's flat and collected her. But within a week, Gloria discharged herself. When Sophie found out, she telephoned Gloria's home and a defensive, slurred voice spoke to her.

"I'm better now dear," Gloria said, "and they get up so early there. And you know how I hate making beds, Meg."

When Sophie asked the doctor at the clinic whether there was anything else she could do to help Gloria, he was blunt with her.

"Sophie, addicts can make everyone around them as sick as

themselves. She won't change now. Take a bit of advice. Get on with your own life. Don't let her drain you."

Reluctantly Sophie agreed. Gloria's addiction was too powerful and there was no chance of her recovering. All she could do now, was to give Gloria as much love and support as she could during her remaining life.

There was another late call, early in December. Gloria's breathing sounded like the wailing of broken bag pipes and her voice rasped out the words in a flat monotone.

"Sophie, we're going to Bermuda for Christmas. I need warm weather to shake off this goddam 'flu. And Sebastian starts a play in March and he needs a suntan for the part. But I'll be back for our birthday."

"Are you getting treatment for your 'flu, Gloria?"

"Yes dear. It's my throat mainly. It gets so sore. What are you doing for Christmas?"

"Well," Sophie said, "I promised to cook lunch for my mother."

Gloria yelled, coughed, and after choking for a while said, "Oh God, Sophie, that's the best laugh I've had in ages."

"And on Boxing Day," Sophie went on, "I'm having lunch with my father and his new live-in girlfriend. She's about eight years younger than me. It's a bit of a strange feeling really."

"God, families. Who'd have families." Gloria wheezed. "I'll think of you at Christmas dear."

"And I'll think of you, Gloria. Take care of yourself, won't you. And I love you."

"And I love you too dear. I'll see you at the Ritz, Sophie."

"See you at the Ritz."

Michael agreed with Sophie. The idea was brilliant. If Gloria had trouble with her throat, what better than a jellyfish for the birthday. Sophie arrived at the hotel early. In her bag, she had a list of clinics where the patients did not have to make their own beds. She hoped that with a bit of luck she could persuade Gloria to try more treatment. Within half an hour all the tables in the Palm Court were occupied. She listened to the sounds of other people's greetings and conversations and checked her watch. It was almost four o'clock. She wondered whether Gloria had found it difficult to slip away from the flat. She picked up the present she had bought for her. It was another silver fish that she'd found in a Bond Street jewellers. It had a much stronger chain than the last one, so it was unlikely that any of Gloria's hectic lovemaking could break it. She waited for her friend, remembering with pleasure their first mad day together in Grafton Street. By five o'clock when there was still no sign of her, Sophie became worried. She could see Michael looking anxiously in her direction. At the risk of Sebastian finding out about their secret birthday teas, she decided to telephone Gloria's home. The housekeeper answered.

"Oh, Miss Smith, I'm afraid Mrs Fielding died this morning. It was all very sudden. She had a choking fit. We called the ambulance but she died before it reached the hospital."

There was more about funeral arrangements and the *Daily Telegraph*, but Sophie was too shocked for them to register.

She returned to the table and sat huddled in the corner. She felt completely lost and didn't know what to do or where to go. Michael approached her and asked whether he should serve tea. She nodded.

"Will it be just for one, Miss Smith?"

"Yes."

"Is your friend unable to get here?"

"Yes," she whispered.

"Nothing serious, I hope."

"I'm afraid so," Sophie said. She couldn't bring herself to

say dead. It was too final. "She passed away this morning Michael."

"Oh dear. The poor lady. I'm so sorry. What a dreadful thing. Are you all right now sitting here?"

"Yes."

Michael did not ask any more questions. The tea was served quickly and efficiently. Each mouthful became a communion with the past. A remembrance of shared times. The sounds of the tea room were muffled like vibrations heard from under the sea. The people slowly departed, leaving Michael as the sole witness to the jelly cake with one candle. Sophie looked down at the translucent cell with its nucleus of light and wished for Gloria's peace as she blew out the flame.

Michael escorted her to the Piccadilly entrance.

"We'll see you again soon I hope Miss. And I'm very sorry about Mrs Fielding."

"Thank you for everything Michael," she said.

She caught a bus to Sloane Square and walked slowly back to Nell Gwynn House. The temperature had dropped and she could feel the damp coldness in her bones. It was Friday the thirteenth, she thought, and a part of her was missing. She felt no tears, no overwhelming sadness, just a great emptiness. She entered the flat, half expecting to hear the telephone ringing and the sound of the hoarse voice once more. But apart from the noise from the central heating, the place was silent. She sat in the dark, reliving past conversations and trying to visualise Gloria's face. Then she remembered the words spoken in the gardens at De Courcy House. She telephoned Sebastian at once. He was polite but obviously irritated by her call.

"Sebastian, please don't be offended, but when Steve died, Gloria told me she wanted to be buried next to him in the double plot near Black Rock. They were married a long time

Sebastian and I know she really did want that. I just wondered whether she'd mentioned it."

Sebastian sighed. "Oh Sophie, don't be such a Catholic. Of course she didn't mention it. She didn't think about anything. She'll be cremated and her ashes scattered. That's my decision. Now, I've got a lot on my mind Sophie. Thank you for your call."

She wept with rage and frustration, unable to accept Sebastian's refusal. She lay on the bed bargaining with God for Sebastian to change his mind, until she fell asleep exhausted by her long list of promises. She woke again at one in the morning after a dream about Steve and Gloria and began pleading her case to an imaginary Sebastian. By three o'clock, after wrestling between faith and anger, she gave in.

"Thy Will Be Done," she said and wondered why it was so easy to say for herself but not for the people she loved.

Her doorbell rang and she froze with fright. Had a miracle happened? Had Sebastian changed his mind and come round to tell her? Feeling slightly insane, she approached the door and peeped through the spyhole. It was her father. She unlocked the door and stared at him madly.

"Dad?"

"Are you on your own?" Bill Rainbow grinned and peered round the door. "I'm not interrupting anything, am I?"

"No, come in," she said.

"I was emptying the fruits tonight and I was just passing when I saw your lights were on. So I thought, why not see Sophie for a coffee before I go home. What's up girl?" He touched her swollen face. "You been crying?"

The warmth and strength of his hug brought back the tears. She poured out the story while he listened sympathetically. At the end of her ranting, he took her by the arm and led her to a chair.

"Now," he said, "you sit down and I'll make the coffee. Got any bickies?"

She listened to him pottering in the kitchenette, sorting out matching saucers and fastidiously laying a tray. It was like being a child again, when he would wipe down Maggie's dirty kitchen table and drink cocoa with her.

"This friend of yours, the American woman," he said heaping sugar into his cup.

"Gloria?"

"Yeah. Well, who gets the money now she's dead?"

"No one. It all goes back to the Trust."

"Does it now." He sipped his coffee thoughtfully.

"Why?" Sophie asked.

"Good punter, your Mr Fielding. Likes to play the tables but he's not very lucky."

"Does he go to Julian's casinos?"

"Oh yeah. Likes to show off to his tarts. Owes us quite a few shillings, does Mr Fielding."

Sophie sighed.

"Anyway, enough about him," Bill said. "Why don't you come and have lunch with us Sunday. You've got to admit my little girl's a blinking marvellous cook. Better than Maggie ever was."

Sophie agreed with him. He talked about the extension he was adding to his house and his plans for a patio. As she listened to his ideas for the garden and his delight about his newly acquired comforts, she wondered what life would have been like if he had not been sent to prison. He recounted gambling stories until she was pleasantly sleepy.

"Right, I'm off now," he said. "It's time you got yourself to bed. Can't have you looking all washed out now, can we? I'll pick you up Sunday, round twelve."

"It's okay Dad, you sleep in. I can make my own way there."

217

She woke up halfway through the afternoon. Heavy with emotional fatigue, she dragged herself into the kitchen to find there was nothing to eat. She had half-an-hour before the store opposite closed. She pulled on some jeans and hurried over. She had been so busy throwing tins into the trolley that she had not noticed Mike. As she waited in the queue, wishing that she had washed and at least cleaned her teeth, she caught sight of him waiting by the checkout. He smiled and she cringed. Why on the one day that she looked like a piece of old rope, did Mike have to turn up?

"You look dreadful," he said as she took her place at the till.

"Thank you," she said.

He took the bags from her and led her across the road. "Will you ask me in for a coffee?"

"I've got eight days dubbing starting Monday and I've got to read my script."

It was all too much, she thought. Everything was coming together too fast. She could feel her bottom lip quivering and her entire body losing control.

"Hey little friend, what's wrong?" he said.

It felt as if her whole face was dribbling. Her nose, her eyes and even her neck seemed to be leaking.

"Gloria died," she sobbed.

Blubbing like a child, she let him lead her back to the flat. She continued bawling while he unpacked the shopping for her.

"It's good to let it all out," he said.

They had baked beans on toast and between sniffles, she told him the whole story.

"When you know the date of the funeral, let me know and I'll come with you. Do you still have my number or have you thrown it away?"

"I threw it away."

He looked at her earnestly. "If I write it down, promise you'll call?"

"Okay. And how's your girlfriend?"

He flinched and looked down at his hands. "She died from an overdose last year."

"I'm sorry Mike," she said.

They held hands, sharing a bond of grief.

When he left, she tried looking at the script but was unable to concentrate. She switched on the television but found her mind wandering through the past days' events. She took a bath and overcome by the soothing warmth fell asleep. She woke in confusion when the telephone rang. Dripping with water and numb with cold, she heard Sebastian's voice apologising for the lateness of the call. His whole attitude towards her had changed. Politely, he explained that he had thought about their previous night's discussion and decided that he would send Gloria's ashes back to Ireland straight after the funeral. Sophie was astounded. It seemed like a miracle, as though her prayers had been answered within twenty-four hours. She lay in bed that night marvelling at the power of prayer.

"I promise to make sure you're with Steve, Gloria," she whispered, and drifted into a contented sleep.

In her dream, Vladimir was waiting for her by the edge of a lake. Rising from the centre of the water was a large, pyramid shaped cake with a burning candle on top. Vladimir offered her his hand and they both drifted across the water towards the light. As they grew closer, the radiant candle changed its shape to that of a fiery being. From the head, there came blinding flames and Sophie shut her eyes in terror. She heard Vladimir's voice say, "Look to the heart of the flame, Sophie. Have faith." She forced herself to look through the fire and found eyes of purest love.

During Sunday lunch, Sophie told Bill about Sebastian's change of heart.

"Well, he didn't have much choice, did he?" he said winking at her.

"How do you mean?" Sophie asked, taking some more Yorkshire pudding.

"Let's say, we worked something out." Bill roared with laughter. "You see, I went round to see him with a couple of lads and we said, 'Either you send the American back to Ireland or we'll take a closer look at your kneecaps.'"

As Sophie poured gravy over her vegetables, she smiled at the strange routes that led to miracles.

Compared to a church, where there are dark corners or pillars behind which one can hide, a crematorium is bright and Sophie felt horribly exposed and vulnerable. Few people were at the funeral. Some photographers were outside and she was glad she was able to cling to Mike's arm. The vicar spoke kindly to the bereaved but obviously had difficulty remembering Gloria's name. Down at the front, Sebastian sang the hymns lustily, while Sophie was unable to utter a sound for fear of sobbing. When the casket disappeared behind the curtains, she pulled her hair over her eyes to soak up the tears. Mike handed her a piece of kitchen roll and she heard the rustle as he crumpled it to his own face. The car was waiting outside to take her back to the studios.

The night plane to Dublin landed in thick fog and it was an hour before the taxi reached the Shelbourne. There was a letter from Vladimir waiting at reception. He was delighted that she was staying in Ireland for a few days and was looking forward to their time together. From her room on the fourth floor, she watched the changing wispy shapes as the fog moved around the trees in Saint Stephen's Green. She thought about Gloria's ashes buried close to Steve and remembered her own first night in the Hibernian, five long years ago when she had been like the creeping thing at the bottom of Vladimir's pond, unconscious of the world. There was so much she wanted to discuss with Vladimir. So much she wanted to share.

By morning, a south west wind had removed the fog and it was a bright, sunny day. Sophie stood on the steps of the hotel watching the cars revving up by the traffic lights. Then she walked along to Dawson Street, where the hotel porter had told her there was a flower shop. Among the vases of beautiful sprays and long stemmed blooms, she found some stately lilies. Their sweet perfume filled the air and their luminous, white, wax-like petals seemed to glow. She asked for one lily and one deep red rose.

The taxi drove through Ballsbridge and Black Rock. The flowers rested on her lap. She kept looking at the soft, milky white petals of the lily. They reminded her of the colour of the moon reflected on a calm sea. They turned on to the road to Bray, passing modern houses and road works until they came to the cemetery. The driver parked just inside the gates.

The sight of so many graves was overwhelming.

She walked along a cemented paveway, passing angels and celtic crosses inscribed with poetry and prayers, until she found the grave. She gazed down at the black marble headstone and the small piece of ground that covered her two great friends. Out of the corner of her eye, she could see the waiting taxi. Wisps of smoke drifted out of the driver's window. She heard the swishing sounds of passing traffic and tinkling echoes from a mason adding an inscription to a stone. The sounds reminded her of the wind rattling through the rigging of the small boats on the beach in Tunisia. She knelt down on the square marble wall enclosing the grave and placed the red rose on the left and lily on the right, then she whispered her gratitude and love.

Through blurred eyes she looked up to the now greying sky. Although the clouds were gathering, she could still feel the brightness of the hidden light. And so it had been with Gloria, she thought. The darkness of her addiction had never removed the inner light. That light had given Sophie the word of life. Vladimir added meaning to that word and now, like a dragonfly stretching its wings, Sophie felt the courage to live it.